Lost Girls

All of them leaned against the boat, trying to push it back up onto the beach. The sand had turned to hard, wet mud, and the boat would not move backwards through it. "Push!" cried Huzzy. "Harder! Harder!"

The tide heard her first and it pulled harder and harder each time Huzzy said the word. Now it was six girls against the power of the great riptide. They could not see each other or the boat or the tide that they and the boat were fighting. Amidst shouts and cries that were carried off by the wind or drowned out by the sound of the rain and the waves, the girls used all their might to save their beloved boat. It was no use. Within minutes the wet sand pulled out from under their feet and the big boat started moving forward . . .

Scholastic Children's Books,
Scholastic Publications Ltd,
7–9 Pratt Street, London NW1 0AE, UK

Scholastic Inc.,
730 Broadway, New York, NY 10003, USA

Scholastic Canada Ltd,
123 Newkirk Road, Richmond Hill,
Ontario, Canada L4C 3G5

Ashton Scholastic Pty Ltd,
PO Box 579, Gosford, New South Wales,
Australia

Ashton Scholastic Ltd,
Private Bag 1, Penrose, Auckland,
New Zealand

First published in the US by Scholastic Inc., 1991
First published in the UK by Scholastic Publications Ltd, 1992

Copyright © Linda Williams Aber, 1991

ISBN 0 590 55071 3

Typeset by Wyvern Typesetting Ltd, Bristol
Printed by Cox & Wyman Ltd, Reading, Berks

10 9 8 7 6 5 4 3 2 1

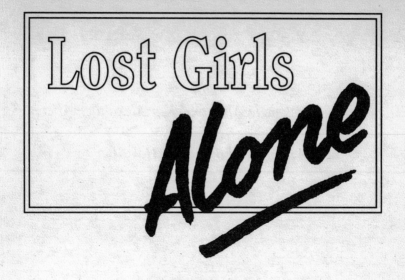

Lost Girls Alone

Linda Williams Aber

Hippo Books
Scholastic Children's Books
London

For
Corey Mackenzie Aber and Kip Alexander Aber

With special thanks to Hal Aber

Preface

It is a small island that does not exist for those who make up the charts used by sailors who sail in and out of the seven hundred Abaco Islands. Covered by island pines and palmettos, this tiny Bahama cay has been deserted for more than two hundred years. The beaches are pure white, the waters are turquoise-blue, and the history of the island is as colourful as the story of the Greek sea captain who was shipwrecked there in a storm and gave the island his name.

Chilas Cay was home to the captain for more than a year after the wreck of his ship *Kayaska*. He survived and left the island the way he found it, deserted. Two hundred years later six girls out for a pleasure cruise got caught in a storm not unlike the storm two centuries before. Now, Chilas Cay is the island home of the lost girls, who wait and watch and hope for the miracle that will bring them home again.

1
The Boat

The thing that squatted in the sand near the turquoise water's edge had begun to look something like a boat, but not like a boat anyone had ever seen before. The sides of the pod-shaped vessel bulged and suddenly were flat, then they bulged again where the great trunks of island pine trees were stacked one on another. The logs were rough, and bark hung in strips and curls, bleached and brittle from the sun. Clumps of dried mud filled the seams where log met log. Twisted plaits of sea-soaked sisal plants made into ropes held the logs together, and the ends of the homemade lines were knotted and left dangling.

It sat beached in a spot that was dangerous because of the way the tide came in. Water rushed in, suddenly deep, in a crisscross pattern that brought with it an undertow strong enough to pull the whole island out with it. Or so it seemed. Coral reefs and jagged volcanic rock ledges formed the cove in which the boat was being built. The treacherous undertow would be put to good use the day the boat was finished and ready to sail. One hard push into the strong grip of the tide would launch it, pulling it away from the island and out to sea.

The sun was directly overhead. The breeze that blew did not cool the air. It only moved it like the hot breath of a dog panting. The building of the boat always had to stop at this hour. No one could stand the noonday heat, even though the six girls had lived on the small deserted island for one hundred and fifteen days. Not even Huzzy Smyth, whose skin was already blacker than any sun could ever burn it. Although this great hope for escape had given the girls the strength to work every day, the sun weakened them when it was hottest. Under such a blazing light, none of them could carry even one more log, tie one more knot, or dart safely away from one more grab from the tide's watery fingers reaching for the ankle that got too close.

"We must stop now, my girls," Huzzy ordered as she usually did at noon. "The tide is getting higher, and the sun is getting hotter. To build a strong boat, we must be strong. Today we have worked enough on this."

Huzzy knew the power of the island sun and the tide. It was the same on all of the Abaco Islands. And although her home island was Green Turtle

The Boat

Cay, she applied the same island customs and wisdom to the life she and her five shipmates had lived since the storm carried their sailing sloop *Sea Breeze* to the reef just offshore of this small, uncharted island known as Chilas Cay. When the sun was highest in the sky, work stopped.

"Come now, Annie," Huzzy said to the youngest in the group. "Lay down your sisal plant leaves now and rest. The boat will wait." The soft lilt of Huzzy's island accent always made the orders she gave easy to take. She had been their skipper on the pleasure cruise that was to have lasted only a week. Annie Southard still remembered the day, almost four months ago, when they first saw Huzzy, standing tall and straight. Annie and the others immediately knew they were in good hands for their first sailing cruise. But a storm had taken their boat out of Huzzy's hands and carried them to this island. They survived, but the *Sea Breeze* sank. Left stranded, they were without hope until the day Huzzy came up with the idea to stop waiting for a boat to come and rescue them. Holding one board from the *Sea Breeze* in her hand, Huzzy had announced the plan to build a new boat and save themselves.

Annie did as she was told. She dropped the dripping sisal leaves from her shoulders and stood back, wiping the salty water from her sunburned skin. Her hair, which had been a colourless blonde-brown when she'd first arrived on the island, was now sun-streaked golden. It flowed over her shoulders and down her back, giving her the look of a wild girl.

Four other wild girls dropped what they were doing, too. They were all deeply tanned and wore pieces of cloth around their waists and tied across their tops. With pink, lavender, and yellow flowers stuck here and there in their hair, the girls looked like a tribe of island princesses instead of the ordinary Florida girls they really were. So much had changed since they'd been lost. The fears that came with them to the island had gradually left as they became more accustomed to their home away from home. The island offered plenty of fruit, fish, and fresh water, so their fears of not surviving because of hunger and thirst went away. The cloth from the sails of the *Sea Breeze* combined with the thick, leafy branches of the palmettos made sturdy enough shelters to shield them from cool night breezes and afternoon rains, so their fears of the elements disappeared also.

New fears replaced the old ones. Fear of the unknown turned to fear of the known as they explored their island and discovered certain dangers. The thick groves of palms, pines, and ferns held more than just fruits and nuts. Amidst the flowering plum trees and under the floor of dried palm leaves were sudden sinkholes that swallowed up the unsuspecting hiker who accidentally stepped in. The daggerlike leaves of the Spanish bayonet plant could slice through skin, leaving deep stripes of blood on any arms or legs that brushed by. Thorny veins wrapped and trapped those who reached for fruit too high on a branch. Poisonous coral sumac offered white fruits that looked good enough to eat, but caused skin rashes bad enough to kill.

In the sea other dangers floated silently, waiting for a leg to wrap around, a foot to stab, an arm to sting. It wasn't only the tide that threatened. Sharp coral fans, startled barracuda, stingrays, and sharks on a hunt for food were cause for caution. On the surface, with its changing colours of turquoise, purple, green, and navy, the water looked like a beautiful invitation to cool comfort. It was, but Huzzy, who knew all the dangers, warned the girls to respect the water and the dense groves of plants and trees. While they offered survival, they did not give up their bounty without threat of a fight.

"If you go to pick fruits," Huzzy had warned, "step carefully and test the ground in front of you before you step down too hard. If you go to find fish, find them first with your eyes and be sure your catch is alone."

Having been warned again and again, the girls had stayed safe so far. They were careful not to explore alone, and they remembered Huzzy's words of caution wherever they were. So, even the real fears didn't make them prisoners of their sleeping mats. They moved about freely for the most part.

But the one fear that would not go away was the fear that they would never see their homes again. It was to counteract this fear that they worked to create the boat. But it was Huzzy who made them stop when the heat made work dangerous.

Annie's sister, Sarah, also obeyed Huzzy. She stopped mixing mud and ground shells, and pushed her waist-length blonde hair out of her face. She squinted as the sun shone into her light blue eyes. Her hands were covered with mud, and she scraped them against the rim of a pot full of the thick stuff. She'd been plugging cracks in the boat's side.

Allison McKinney came around from the other side, her face smeared with the same mud. Without realizing, she added more of it to her cheek when she used the back of her hand to push a strand of her long, wavy brown hair out of her mouth. The mud hardly showed against her tanned skin, but her green eyes stood out like a cat's in the dark as she looked up to be sure the sun was really directly over them. She didn't want to work one minute more than she had to. It was definitely easier to watch for a boat to come than to make one.

Another younger girl climbed out of the pod. A bushy bunch of orange hair caught in a faded elastic band appeared first. All that hair standing up so high made Libby Hunt look taller than her twelve years had made her. Her legs needed to be longer, though, to easily swing over the side of the boat. "I need some help getting out," she said to the others down on the sand.

Sarah offered up a muddy hand, and Libby took it. For a second Libby felt dizzy, maybe from the sun, maybe from standing up too fast. She dropped down onto the sand and fell back. She was the one the water had been waiting for. It reached for her feet and pulled the sand out from under them. For a second she knew *she* was next. Her eyes blurred from the dizzy spell, and she was sure she saw a giant watery hand coming out of the ocean to dig its claws into her and carry her back with it. She screamed and it all went away, the dizziness, the blurred vision, the watery claw.

"It's all right, Libby," Sarah's soft voice was saying. "I've got you."

"What did you think, anyway?" Allison said in her usual sarcastic tone. "That the tide got you?" Then she laughed at how silly that was.

Huzzy saw the look of dazed fear on Libby's freckled face and put an arm around her. "It was hard work this morning," she said. "Perhaps you did too much today."

Libby came out of her daze. "But we're so close to being finished, aren't we, Huzzy?" she said hopefully. "We all want to keep going."

"Well, not *all*," said Allison. "I'm worn out. I couldn't lift even another fingerful of mud." She stood picking mud out from under her fingernails, then examined them as though she'd just had a manicure.

"Hoh," Huzzy's deep laugh came out. "I am afraid, Libby, we still have some work ahead before we will be able to call her finished."

"It'll be hard to tell when it's finished, won't it?" Annie asked. "I mean it'll never look like a real boat no matter what we do to it."

"Looks aren't everything," Allison drawled.

The rest of the girls just looked blankly at Allison. Coming from her, a statement like that was laughable, since they all knew looks were everything to Allison. The only thing she cared more about than how she looked was how others *thought* she looked! Of all the girls, Allison had taken the longest to adjust. She had arrived carrying the most luggage, filled with the most useless items: fancy shoes, dressy dresses, and a case full of make-up that she'd insisted on wearing until every last bit of it had been used up. While her stormy relationship with her mother perhaps made leaving home easiest for Allison, leaving her things at home was most difficult for her.

"It is true, Allison," agreed Huzzy. "Looks are not everything. If she floats, if she sails, this is what matters." Huzzy stood back to see if she really meant what she said. Certainly it lacked style and beauty. Secretly she wondered what her father might say if he were ever able to see this hulking thing they were calling a boat. She knew he would be proud of how she had put her knowledge to good use. Huzzy had paid attention when she and her father stood in the open buildings where boats were made on the nearby island of Man-O-War. She had listened to many tales told by the builders whose fathers and grandfathers had also built boats. She knew that timbers were soaked in sea-water to prevent worms and to make the wood easier to cut. But for her boat, there were no smoothly cut timbers. There were only tree trunks that had taken weeks to cut with the small axe they had. Dragging heavy logs through the clearing, across the sand to where the tide came farthest and fastest, took the strength and might of all six girls. Weeks of hard labour had resulted in the strangest-looking boat Huzzy had ever seen built.

What would her father say? She tried to imagine, and his deep, strong voice filled her head. "Huzzy girl," he might say, looking at the fat and awkward vessel, "what shall we say you have made here? Can we call it a boat?" And perhaps he would laugh the same deep and hearty laugh he had passed on to his daughter.

Or maybe he would simply say, "Well, my Huzzy girl, I think you have given your girls two things really. One is a boat, and the other is hope."

How she missed her father's hands on her face when he took her chin in them and spoke straight into her velvet black eyes. She and her father were two of a kind. Both were born to the islands. Both were born to the sea. He was not with her now, but his wisdom always found her when she looked for it.

Now Huzzy did as her father would have if he'd been there. She looked over the work done by the girls this day and examined it with a keen eye for detail. Sarah, Annie, Libby, and Allison stood together and waited to hear what she would say. But one girl stayed apart from the group and didn't seem to pay attention to what any of the others were saying or doing.

Shawn Kallin sat in the sand twisting sisal into ropes. In her hand she held one thick plait that didn't look too different from her own two plaits of long brown hair. She worked carefully and slowly, taking a few minutes every once in a while to make a mental note of the colours of the water and the sky. As she always did after a morning of working on the boat, Shawn would spend the afternoon sketching and painting scenes of the girls and their life on the island. Her eye caught Huzzy walking around the boat, rubbing her fingers over the mud mixture that oozed where it was freshly shoved into cracks. She watched as Huzzy felt the sisal ropes to see if they had soaked long enough to stay flexible. Finally, Huzzy pulled her flat, pink palm over the board that would be the rudder. This was one board they had cut from a log. It had been Shawn's job to work the wood until it was smooth. Shawn held her breath slightly and waited for Huzzy's reaction to her work.

"This board needs more rubbing," she said to Shawn. "A couple more, maybe three days still to go on it. The unevenness could cause it to weaken when the ocean pushes hard against it. A few more days should do it, I think."

Shawn just nodded. It didn't matter to her if the board needed a hundred more days of rubbing. She was in no rush to leave. From the moment the warm winds first breathed in her face, Shawn had felt at home on the island. She often thought of her real home and of her parents who were both artists. She missed them and knew they missed her, too. But they had taught her to live life as though every day was an adventure. If they could see the beautiful colours and textures of the island, Shawn felt sure they would be pleased that her adventures had taken her here. And if they could see the wall of drawings and paintings that lined the inside of her sailcloth shelter walls, she knew they would be proud to see that their talents belonged to her, too.

Shawn stood up and threw the rope plait over the side of the boat. She took the rudder board from Huzzy and felt the wave in it that Huzzy felt. She was right. It did need more work. "I'll get it right, Huzzy," she said. "Don't worry."

Huzzy wasn't worried. She knew her faith in the girls was deserved. Each had her own way about her. Sarah was so organized and motherly. She cooked and comforted and was more responsible than most thirteen-year-old girls should be.

Libby was the happy one who tried to see the cheerful side of every situation. She hid her history well behind her freckle-faced smile and giggles. Even though her parents had been killed in a car accident when she was only eight, Libby's aunt Alice had helped her through the roughest times. Fear was Libby's worst enemy, but her will to be brave was strong.

Annie was just Annie, and Huzzy knew she could count on her to be sensible, calm, and full of quick insights. Having a sister as beautiful as Sarah had made the plainer, younger girl quite realistic. She knew she was plain. She knew she would never be beautiful, but she didn't expect much and so wasn't disappointed often. In fact, Annie didn't want to be like Sarah. She found Shawn much more interesting.

Huzzy looked over at Shawn. Yes, Shawn had a way about her, too. Huzzy had noticed right away that Shawn watched her carefully. And she'd seen that Shawn was the one who fitted the island almost as well as she herself did. Even though she'd separated herself from the others when she built her shelter far down the beach from them, the bond that existed between her and Huzzy overcame the distance. Huzzy really was an island girl. Shawn wanted to be one.

And Allison. Huzzy couldn't help but shake her head and smile when she thought of Allison's ways. She'd been stubborn since the second she stepped on board the *Sea Breeze*. That stubbornness continued on the island when at first she refused to unpack her belongings because she was sure rescuers would be there any minute. Then any day. Then any week. That stubbornness annoyed them all at times, but Huzzy knew it was also what made Allison able to stand up to the dreadful experience of being lost. She was too stubborn to give in to it.

A big clump of mud dried and dropped off the side of the boat and took Huzzy's attention away from her own thoughts. Since it was her mud that had fallen, Sarah picked it up and tried to stick it back in the crack. It was too dried out. "I think I need a little more water," Sarah said, starting to go for some where the tide was now foaming at the mouth of the cove.

"No! Don't!" Libby shouted suddenly. As soon as she'd heard the word *water* the tide's claw came back to her mind.

"Yes," Huzzy agreed. "It is better not to go near the water now. Just to be safe. We will come back here tomorrow morning and work some more, yes?"

"Well, am I the only one who's hungry?" Annie asked, changing the subject abruptly.

Sarah laughed and felt grateful to her younger sister for mentioning food. Talk of the tide made her uncomfortable, but food was the cosiest topic she knew. "I hope you're not the only one who's hungry, Annie," Sarah said. "I have a special surprise for lunch today."

Allison groaned. Sarah was always cooking, which would have been just fine with Allison if there was ever anything *good* to cook. The boat supplies had run out long ago, but Huzzy had shown Sarah how to make all kinds of stews and soups from the conch, fish, and crabs they took from the sea. When Allison thought about all the things she missed from home, tomato ketchup was up there on the list next to boys, shopping, and make-up. Tomato ketchup would have at least made some of Sarah's fish dishes taste like chips. The thought of a big bag of chips from the burger bar made hunger hit her in the stomach. "Well, what's the surprise? And don't say fish fondue."

"Or mud pie," Annie said, looking at her sister's mud-covered hands.

"Only for you, Anniekins," Sarah teased. "But for the rest of us I've made wild cherry soup."

"Cherry soup!" Allison spluttered. "Oh, sick!"

"It will be delicious, Sarah. I am certain of it," Huzzy said before the blonde girl could feel hurt. "Let's go and have it, shall we?" She turned towards the rocks that formed one wall of the cove and climbed to the top. The others followed her up and waited for Huzzy to lead the way down and back to the camp in a clearing where the tree line met the sand. She allowed the others to go first, lending a hand to each on her way down.

Annie practically skipped over the jagged clusters of purple rock. Sarah was more graceful and deliberate with her steps. Allison clucked her tongue with annoyance as she broke a mud-caked nail on a jagged edge. And Shawn seemed to float on the hot breeze that blew over the cliff.

Only Libby stopped at the top and stood with Huzzy. Her red hair stood out like the flames in a wildfire as the breeze fanned it. She wanted to keep going, but her fear of the tide made her look back. From high above the swirling water, Libby got a better look at her tormentor. It looked more olive than turquoise, and the bubbling foam that capped the hurrying waves seemed venomous. She was glad to be high up and out of its reach. Just then a bigger wave ran up the sand and crashed against the bow of the boat, sending a spray of water across Libby's face. "It can reach me," Libby muttered to herself. "Even here it can reach me."

"Hoh!" laughed Huzzy, not knowing what Libby was saying to the wind. "It got you that time, yes?"

Libby didn't answer. She only hurried to climb past Huzzy and down to the safe side where the water only kissed ankles instead of grabbing them. Huzzy looked down and saw Libby hurrying to catch up with Sarah, who automatically put a comforting arm around the girl's shoulder. Left alone on the rocks, Huzzy took one look back at the boat. It was so close to the edge of the watermark on the sand, and that last wave had moved the mark around both sides of the bow. It had to be that close. Huzzy knew that even six girls pushing at once were going to have a hard time moving such a big body of wood and mud. The boat would be no good to anyone if they couldn't get it into the water. She was counting on the pull of the tide to help her when she needed it. And the boat? Well, the boat she was just counting on to save the lives of six lost girls.

2
Danger

Each afternoon when work on the boat stopped and lunch was finished, Shawn went alone to her shelter. It stood out like a welcome oasis on a dry desert, with the white sailcloth tent draped from the branches of a red-flowering plum tree. Tiny hummingbirds flitted about, darting from flower to flower, drinking nectar from the blossoms.

Shawn had painted pink and lavender bouquets on the flaps of her tent. Those colours were echoed by the sun-bleached conch shells that formed a wall around her shelter. This was her counting wall. She'd laid down two shells on the second night on the island, and every night thereafter all the girls gathered at the wall before supper to watch Shawn add another shell, one for each day on their home away from home.

As the wall had grown, so had Shawn's collection of drawings and paintings. At first she sketched the girls on the *Sea Breeze* feeding the gullies, looking out at the sunset, and sailing happily on the open sea. Then came the wreck, and the sketches captured the sunken *Sea Breeze*, the stranded girls, and the natural beauty of their island. Every event, every change showed up in Shawn's sketched and painted record of the preceding one hundred and fifteen days. When the paper of her sketch pads was used up, she found other things on which to paint. Smooth rocks, flat shells, leaves the size of elephant ears, and scraps of sailcloth provided textured surfaces that added a part of the island itself to her pictures of it.

Shawn had chosen a ragged-edged board broken off the *Sea Breeze* wreckage as the "canvas" on which to paint a picture of the boat they were building. Since Huzzy had used one board from the *Sea Breeze* to start the new boat, Shawn thought it was appropriate for her painting to start with a board from it, too. The board was about three feet across and two feet high, making this her largest work. She'd carefully peeled off the fibreglass fabric covering, leaving a smooth, fine-grained surface that took paint well. The background of the painting was finished. The top half of the board was a deep, periwinkle-blue, powdered with puffs of billowy, white clouds. The sky met turquoise water that flowed towards a pink-beige sandy beach. Outlined in the centre of the board was a large pod-shaped thing, the boat.

Shawn stood back from it, looking for what needed to be done next. Annie's voice startled her, but she wasn't sorry to hear it. "It's going to be beautiful, Shawn," Annie said, seeing the partially finished painting for the first time. "You paint the colours of the water and sky so perfectly."

"I'm afraid this will be the last painting that matches so well," Shawn answered, putting the pointed end of the paintbrush in her mouth and closing one eye to check the proportion of the boat to the waves that washed up to it. "My paints have just about run out."

"Oh, no," Annie said, feeling really sorry. She knew that Shawn's paintings were as important to her as food. Once she had told Annie that in her family books, music, and art were the bread and water of life. "But do you have enough to finish this painting? It's going to be so beautiful when it's done. It's your best one yet, I think," said Annie sincerely.

"Well, it's my *biggest* one yet," Shawn said. "I *have* to finish it." Then almost to herself, she said it again, "I *have* to finish it."

Annie looked over at the shelf Shawn had made from rocks. It was her art supplies shelf, and at first it had been filled with coloured pencils, pads of paper, brushes, and small tubes of acrylic paint. In the days on the island, those tubes of paint had been turned into pictures, beautiful pictures that covered every inch of the tent wall and were piled on the palm mat floor. When the girls were finally rescued, the pictures would tell the story of the lost girls in great detail, thought Annie.

"How will you finish if you don't have any more paint?" Annie asked.

Shawn looked thoughtfully around at her work and tried to think of an answer to Annie's question. Her eyes found the arrangement of rock paintings she'd made. Those had been the first solution to the no-paper problem. She remembered the panic she felt when she'd torn off the last page from the pad. But on a walk across the beach five flat stones lay washed up in a small seaside pool. As soon as she saw them, Shawn knew paper wasn't the only surface to paint on. An idea came to her now and Annie could practically see discovery in her eyes.

"What is it, Shawn?" asked Annie curiously.

"Paint!" Shawn answered, her yellow-brown eyes lighting up.

"Where?"

"Everywhere," Shawn said. "All around us. In the leaves, in the fruits, in the petals of the flowers, the seaweed, everywhere!"

"You mean, you'll make it!" Annie exclaimed excitedly.

"Exactly. And if you like, you can help me find

it." Shawn was excited, too. In fact, she didn't want to waste even a minute. "Let's go now," she said. "We'll start in the palmetto groves and make our way to the other side of the island. I bet we'll find plenty of different things to try. After we collect enough we'll experiment to see what colours we can make."

Annie could hardly wait to get started. She felt so happy to be included in Shawn's plans. From the day she'd met the exotic-looking girl, Annie liked her and Shawn liked Annie. Even though Shawn was fourteen and Annie was only eleven, they got along well. Everything about Shawn was interesting to Annie, from her double-pierced ear to her incredible artistic talents to her strange attachment to the island that was their beautiful prison. "I'm ready," she said enthusiastically.

It was a rule that anyone leaving the shelter and camp area must tell Huzzy where she was going, so everyone was accounted for at all times. The island was small enough to walk across in an hour, but the length of it stretched two miles, and a walk through the thick growth of vines, tangled brush, and trees could take many hours. The dangers that Huzzy had warned of were real, so it was important for the group to keep track of one another's whereabouts.

Shawn picked up a cup and a rounded rock and said, "Now I'm ready, too. We'll use this to try grinding different things to see what colours come out."

Annie was fascinated by Shawn's idea. She knew she'd never be able to paint like Shawn could, but it would be wonderful to be able to help make the paints Shawn used. "I'll run back and tell Huzzy we're going," Annie said, starting to go.

"Doesn't she know you're here?" Shawn asked. She was eager to get started and didn't want to waste time.

"Well," Annie said thoughtfully, "I did tell Sarah I was coming over to see you, so I suppose that's good enough."

"Of course it is," Shawn assured her. "We won't go too far. Just into the groves on this end of the island. We've all explored there before. And besides, as long as we're together we're not breaking any rules, really. The main thing is always to be with someone else." She picked up a plastic bag and turned to go.

"OK," Annie agreed. "Then we're off."

The two girls went behind Shawn's tent, stepped across the counting wall, and into the thick brush. They stepped carefully, as Huzzy had taught them all to do, and pushed vines and branches away from their eyes. Shawn was right. They didn't have to go far to find some things from which to try making paint. Right away they came across a jumbay tree that offered a few colours to try. While the flowers were white, the pods that hung from the branches were a richly coloured brown. Shawn picked one off and ground it in her cup. It powdered easily, and when it was moistened with the juice from the flowers it made a thick paste.

"Gather some of these pods, Annie," Shawn ordered excitedly. "I can't believe how well this is going to work!"

Behind the jumbay tree was a beautiful patch of turk's cap mallow, a shrub covered with bright crimson flowers. "There's your red!" Annie said, claiming the discovery as her own. "And look! Purple!" She was pointing to a pokewood plant with purple buds and a deep red-purple stalk.

The two hunters picked samples of all the different plants and flowers they saw, with one discovery leading to the next. They noticed every blossom, every stalk, every berry. What they didn't notice was how very deep into the island jungle they were going. Shawn moved through the tangle of trees with ease, and Annie followed, feeling safe with the older girl who was so at home anywhere on the island. When their collecting bag was nearly full, hunger took their attention away from the search for more paint sources. Instead they took a break to search for fruit.

"Over there, Annie," Shawn said, pointing to a tree heavy with ripe, red plums. "Follow me."

With Annie right behind her, Shawn led the way across a clearing. She stopped to examine a small plant that grew close to the ground. The petals of the flower were white and the middle of it was a bright orange, perfect for a painting of a sunset. While she bent down to pick a few of the pretty flowers, Annie went around her and kept her eyes on a plum that hung on a low branch.

Just as Annie leaned and reached for the fat, juicy fruit, Shawn shouted out a frightened warning, "Look out! The bayonet leaves!" The sharp, bladelike leaves of the Spanish bayonet plant flashed at Annie's legs, but Shawn's quick warning made her jump to the side. The blades seemed to miss her, but in her jump a sinkhole got her. The ground gave way under both feet, and before Annie or Shawn knew what was happening, Annie began to feel herself being sucked down into the earth.

"Shawn!" she screamed, reaching out her hands for help. No amount of pulling up with her feet would release them from the tight hold the quicksand of the sinkhole had on her. "Help me!" she cried. Tears streamed down her face and at the same time lines of blood formed on one of her arms. The bayonet blades had cut her there, after all, and the sight of the sudden bleeding made Annie scream in a terrified squeal.

Shawn was quick to drop the bag she carried and

run to Annie's outstretched hands. She pulled on her, but Annie was now up to her knees and still sinking. The more she cried and struggled and fought against the pull of the hole, the faster it took her. Vines hanging from a nearby tree seemed the only answer. Shawn grabbed for one and pulled on it to make sure it was really attached. It wasn't. The thick, snakelike rope came off in her hands. She dropped it and reached for the next one. One strong pull on it proved it was connected. "Take this, Annie!" Shawn cried. "Hold onto it and don't let go no matter what!"

Annie reached out and grabbed the vine. Her tears blurred everything, and her own cries made it difficult for her to hear what Shawn was saying next. "Tie this one around you!" Shawn was shouting. "Stay still! Don't move! Just try to stay still, and I think you'll stop sinking."

Annie couldn't tie anything. Her hands shook, making it impossible for her to use them. It took all her strength to try to stop the shaking, but she knew Shawn was right. She had to stay perfectly still. "Please, Shawn," she cried. "Don't let me sink any more. *You* tie the vine. Please. *You* tie it. Please. Please. *Please!*"

Annie's cries were desperate, and Shawn's reaction was immediate. She took another sturdy vine and carefully reached around Annie's waist with it. Her own foot touched the edge of the sinkhole, and she felt her toe start to go. She pulled it back in time and finished knotting the heavy vine around Annie. Then she pulled it to take all the slack out and wrapped the slack around a shrub. Now there was a tight grip holding Annie at the waist to prevent her from going deeper.

"Annie," Shawn tried to say over her cries. "Annie, you've got to listen to me. I'll have to go for help."

Annie panicked. "Don't leave me! Please! Don't leave me here! They'll come looking for us. They'll be here in a minute, I'm sure. Don't leave me!" Her crying turned to begging sobs.

"Annie," Shawn reasoned, "they won't know where to look. They'll have no idea where to look. We didn't tell them where we were going." Huzzy's rule came back to her mind, and her mistake stood out like the blood on Annie's arm.

Shawn decided to try pulling on the vine that was wrapped around Annie's waist. Maybe if she pulled hard enough she could just yank her out. "I'm going to pull, Annie," she explained, "and you try to lean up and out of the hole." Shawn slowly started hauling.

"Stop!" Annie cried. "Don't pull! When you pull it's like something pulls my legs even harder. Just stop, please."

"Oh, Annie," Shawn said, tears falling on her cheeks now, too. "Don't worry. We'll get you out.

Don't worry. I won't leave you. I won't leave you." She reached her hand across the sinkhole and held Annie's hand. Shawn felt as stuck as Annie. As long as the girl was in the hole, she had no choice but to just stay with her and wait. She was afraid if she left her and went for help, Annie would start moving again and sink even more, maybe even completely. "I won't leave you, Annie," she said again.

Annie's crying came and went and came again. In the moments when she stopped crying, Shawn called out, hoping the others had made the discovery that she and Annie were missing. "Huzzy!" Shawn shouted through the jungle.

No answer. No sound other than the birds talking among themselves.

"Huzzy! Huzzy!" Shawn called out again. When no answer came, Annie felt even more stuck, so Shawn didn't call out for a while. She tried to keep Annie's mind occupied and fed her plums from the tree that had started their trouble in the first place. She assured her that even though she'd said before no one would know where to look, Huzzy would find them.

While they waited, Shawn tried other ways of releasing Annie from the sucking sand. With a stick she tried pushing the sandy mud away from Annie's legs. A mysterious force pulled the stick from her hands, and the two girls watched in silent horror as it disappeared almost instantly.

Shawn looked up and tried to see sky through the cover of palmetto branches. She could hardly believe her eyes when she saw it was as orange as the centre of the flower she'd bent to pick earlier that afternoon. Had so many hours passed that the sun was already setting? If that was true, darkness would not be far behind. She had to try calling out again. "Huzzy!" her voice echoed through the silent jungle.

"Huzzy!" Annie's voice called out, too.

"Huzzy! Huzzy!" they shouted together.

They waited and listened, but all they could hear were the sounds of the evening settling in. Suddenly the silence was cracked by a tiny sound. They listened and heard it again.

"Annie?" a voice was saying.

"Shawn?" another voice followed from far away.

"Sarah!" shouted Annie, suddenly unable to hold her voice in or her body still. The movement made her sink another inch, but she shouted out again. "Sarah! We're here!"

"Shawn! Annie!" came Huzzy's deep voice through the thick wall of ferns. "Are you there? Where are you, my girls?"

Now Shawn and Annie heard branches crackling under fast-moving feet, and they called out in the direction of the sounds. "Huzzy, we're here!"

Shawn called out with relief. "Over here! Can you see us?"

"I see them!" Annie shouted, new tears forming, but this time happy ones.

When Huzzy and Sarah came breaking through the brush, the reunion was immediately joyous, but Huzzy saw right away that they had some serious trouble to deal with.

"Oh, my Annie," she said. "What has happened to you, my poor girl? Quickly, we must get you out."

"But how?" Shawn asked. "Every pull makes it worse. Every movement makes her sink deeper."

Huzzy moved fast to find a fallen trunk of a tree, which she then rolled to the sinkhole. It fitted over the opening of the hole. "Lie down now, Annie," Huzzy instructed. "Put your body over the log and lie down."

Annie carefully held the vine around her waist and laid her body across the log. When her weight was shifted that way she felt an immediate release on the grip around her legs. Huzzy reached over and, to Shawn's and Annie's amazement, pulled her easily from the hole.

Sarah rushed to her sister's side and threw her arms around her. "Oh, my Anniekins, why didn't you tell us you were going off? We looked everywhere for you."

"It was my fault," Shawn answered. "We didn't

plan to go far. Well, we didn't plan for any of this, really. I'm sorry, Huzzy. Really I am, but I'm so glad you found us."

"And that is the most important thing now," Huzzy said, knowing she didn't have to say any more. The lesson had been learned, she was sure of that. "I am sure your legs must feel tired now, Annie, but it is better if we leave here as quickly as possible before the darkness makes our way more difficult."

With relief flooding over her and giving her new strength, Annie was more than ready to go back to camp. "But we have to bring everything we collected, Shawn," she remembered, looking around for the bag. "At least you'll have the paints you need."

Shawn looked at Annie's legs. They were red from rubbing against the gritty sand that had sucked up to them for the past few hours. Her arms were striped with blood. The dangers of the island had got Annie, but somehow the island had left Shawn alone. Shawn didn't mean to have such a strange thought, but there it was: The island likes me best.

The walk back to camp was quick because no one was looking for anyone or anything. Sarah led the way, followed by Shawn, then Annie, then Huzzy. As she walked behind Annie and noticed the blood dried on her arm where the bayonet leaves had sliced her, Huzzy felt stabbed, too, by worry. So far they'd all been lucky and no one had got sick or been hurt. Now Huzzy thought perhaps they'd all become careless, making it likely that more accidents would occur.

Huzzy shuddered when she thought of Annie sinking lower and lower into that hole. First the *Sea Breeze* had been swallowed by the sea, now the earth had tried to gulp down Annie. Huzzy wondered when the appetite of the island would be satisfied, and she suddenly felt that getting away from the island was urgent. The boat had to be finished soon. It *had* to be.

"Where were you? What happened? What's that all over your legs? What happened to your arm, Annie? You're bleeding!" Libby's questions poured out in a panicked flood of words that held the returning group back for a moment.

Annie's reaction was to burst into tears again, making Libby think things were even worse. "Annie! What's happened to you?" Libby said, her own tears falling now, too.

"It is all right now, Libby," Huzzy said, trying to calm both crying girls. "Annie and Shawn are safe, and we have our group together again."

Over a dinner of conch meat stew Annie told the story between bites and tears.

"You mean to tell me," Allison snapped, "you

ended up in quicksand just because Shawn wanted paint?"

Shawn looked coolly at Allison. "And I suppose if the search had been for make-up it would have been worth it."

"I wanted to go." Annie defended Shawn quietly.

"The main thing is that you're back safely," said Sarah in her most motherly voice. "A good sleep will make us all feel better. Tomorrow's another day."

"Don't remind us," snarled Allison. "Tomorrow's another day, and the next day's another day, and the day after that —"

"That is enough now, Allison," Huzzy stopped her. She could see that the afternoon's events had shortened tempers. "Tomorrow *is* another day," she agreed, "but it is another day that will bring us closer to finishing the boat. It is another day that will bring us closer to home."

"Oh, do you really think that's true, Huzzy?" Sarah cried. "Girls, did you hear that? Tomorrow is another day closer to home." She put her arms around the shoulders of Libby and Annie and pulled them close to her as she savoured the happy thought of home.

Allison turned her eyes out to the ocean where she always looked in hope of seeing a real boat, one that was already built, coming to rescue them.

Danger

As usual the horizon was dotted only with birds, but she didn't stop looking.

Claiming tiredness as her reason for leaving them, Shawn grabbed her bag and hurried up the beach to her white oasis. She looked at the orange-pink evening sky and saw that it still held enough light by which to work. In a race with the sunset, she emptied her bag and found the brown pods. With the rounded stone she crushed the pods to a cocoa-coloured powder and added water to it, making a thick paintlike paste. By what little light was left she looked at her painting that had only the outline of the boat against a background of sky, water, and beach. When the boat was finished it would carry them all away from that beautiful periwinkle-blue and turquoise and sandy pink-beige. She started to dip her brush into the brown paint, but she stopped. She just wasn't ready to finish the boat and leave the island yet.

3
Another Day

Morning crept up, but it didn't surprise Huzzy. She'd been waiting for it with her eyes wide open. As far back as she could remember, Huzzy had never missed a morning's arrival. On her island home, out at sea with her father, or on this empty island with five other girls, her eyes were always the first to see night slowly turn around and become day. The change was one of Huzzy's favourite events, and as her father often said, "It is free, Huzzy girl. Take it!" So she did try to take it, every day.

Her girls were still sleeping, and Huzzy was glad. The work of building the boat the morning before, then the excitement of Annie's accident had exhausted them all. Huzzy, too, would have slept longer if she could have, but she was worried. It wasn't just the long, thin cuts on Annie's arms or the deep purple bruises that appeared on her legs that concerned Huzzy. It was the thought of luck running out, or of carelessness seeping in, that told her she had to do whatever she could to get them all safely off the island and back to their homes.

She lay on her stomach with her smooth chin resting on two fists piled up. The sun was just beginning to shine through the dusty grey-blue veil of mist that hung over the ocean. Sunbeams danced on the choppy waves, and the tide flowed into shore softly, gently. From her shelter on the other side of the kitchen camp area she could see that the home fires still had a good hour of light left in them. Allison had done her job of keeping them fuelled enough to last through the night. Since the first day on the island, home fires had been built along the beach in front of the tree line and their shelters. If a boat or plane passed by in the night, they hoped the fires would attract some attention. Huzzy watched the embers glow and crumble to ashes. One by one the fires went out, but sunlight took over for them. Still, the girls did not stir. At last, Huzzy decided it would be best to wake them so that work on the boat could begin. In the semi-darkness of early morning, she dressed in a swimming costume and flowered sarong wrap, and then she woke the others.

"Good morning, my girls!" she called out in her cheerful island accent. "It looks to be a beautiful day. A perfect day, in fact, to start our work."

Moans and groans came from the three sleeping mats closest to each other. Sarah, Annie, and Libby all pulled covers up over their heads to keep the morning and Huzzy's hearty voice out.

Huzzy laughed at the three sleepyheads. "Come now, my girls. The morning is here to greet you. Do not keep it waiting." How many times had her father said that to her? Every morning he'd come to wake her, saying that. Then when he saw Huzzy was already awake he'd throw his head back and laugh at himself for thinking that maybe just this once his Huzzy would sleep later than he did.

"How can it be morning already?" a muffled voice came from under Libby's cover. "Didn't we just go to sleep?"

Annie peeped out of her cover and saw the home fires just dying out. "It *can't* be morning, but I suppose it must be."

"Yes," said Huzzy. "There is work to be done, and the sooner we are all up and at it the better."

"Well, we aren't *all* up," Annie said. "Look at Allison. You couldn't wake her if you flew jets right by her ears."

"I'm awake. I'm awake," Allison said through a yawn and a stretch. "But the question is, why am I? It's practically the middle of the night, isn't it?"

Now the others all laughed because the sun was definitely on the way up, and the morning's darkness was nothing like the black, black darkness of night.

With Huzzy hurrying them along, the girls dragged themselves out of their covers and dressed for the day on the beach. Sarah was first to be ready and went to the kitchen area to start breakfast. She and Libby had arranged everything in a horseshoe shape with the fireplace at the top of the U and supplies of fruit, dried fish, and fresh water on either side. The dishes from the *Sea Breeze* were stacked as neatly as they had been on board the boat, and their cheerful red-and-white design with the Windswept Sailing Cruises sailing boat on them gave the kitchen a touch of civilization.

Sarah started a fire in the fireplace and reached for a pot to fill with fresh water. When she lifted the jug of water it felt too light. "Oh, darn," she said. "We're out of water again."

"I'll get more for us," Libby volunteered. "Want to come, Annie?"

The path to the freshwater pool they'd discovered the first day on the island was clear and easy to walk on. Huzzy had already checked it for sinkholes and poisonous plants. It was a safe path. Even so, after her experience in the groves yesterday, Annie hesitated.

Sarah saw Annie's worried look and saved her. "I'll go with you, Libby," she said. "Annie, you start cutting up the fruit, and we'll be back quickly."

Every once in a while Annie liked her sister a lot. It was true that her perfect looks, her perfect smile, her perfect personality, and her perfect behaviour usually made Sarah irritating to Annie, but Sarah meant well. Right now, Annie was just grateful that Sarah was going back into the groves to the water pool instead of her. She watched as Libby and her sister walked hand in hand through the fan-shaped leaves of the palmettos. Annie rubbed her sore legs as she remembered how the sinkhole had sucked them down deep.

On their way to the freshwater pool, Libby and Sarah took more care than usual on the familiar path. Even though they didn't really expect surprises, they still looked for them. When they reached the shaded pool both girls laughed with relief.

"We made it!" Libby said.

"Well, of course we did," Sarah said, kneeling by the pool and dipping the empty container into the cool water.

The gurgling sound it made going into the jug made Libby thirsty. She picked up one of the empty cups that was always left by the side of the pool and dunked it into the water. Thirstily she took a big swallow and saw two eyes looking right up the bridge of her nose and into her eyes. Her screams terrified Sarah, who dropped the water jug and looked to see what terrible danger had overtaken Libby.

The screams also brought Huzzy, Allison, and Annie hurrying down the path.

"I drank a lizard!" Libby screamed. "It was in the cup and I drank it!"

Huzzy looked down where Libby had thrown her cup and saw a small green lizard still sitting on the handle. It didn't move. It seemed stunned and terrified by the noise coming from the girl who had just thrown it down to the ground. Huzzy laughed. "Hoh, Libby, look!" she said, pointing to the frightened thing. "It seems you did not drink the little thing, but certainly you have scared him a bit."

"Me? Scared him?" Libby spluttered. Then she looked at the lizard and saw that it was really much smaller than it had looked up close and peeping out of her cup.

Huzzy picked up the cup with the lizard on it and held it out to Libby to look at. At first Libby turned her head away. Huzzy continued to hold it out. Libby shyly looked again and saw the lizard sitting still as a stone.

"I suppose it is quite cute," Sarah said, bravely leaning in a little to take a closer look. And that was exactly when the lizard chose to jump from the cup to Sarah's hair.

Now Sarah's screams brought Shawn running down another path that went from her shelter to the pool. She got there expecting to see snakes the size of fire hoses or perhaps another sinkhole gulping down another girl. Instead, all she saw was a tiny green lizard shaking in Huzzy's hand.

"Thank goodness," Shawn said.

Sarah laughed at herself a little. But Libby couldn't erase the chilling feeling of the lizard's eyes looking straight into her own. Already she could feel her mind filing away the feeling to be brought back in a nightmare.

Huzzy gently placed the wild thing down on a fern leaf, and it gradually disappeared as it turned the exact colour of the leaf. "There are probably billions of those things all around us," Allison said.

"Thanks for telling us," Annie said. "We needed something else to worry about, didn't we, Libby?"

"No, my girls," Huzzy said reassuringly. "The tiny lizard is not something to worry about. My Mama Selina used to sing a song about this lizard, and if you know the song perhaps when you see one it will make you feel happy instead of worried."

"Sing it to us, Huzzy," Libby begged. All of Huzzy's songs had a special meaning to Huzzy, and she passed them on to the girls so they could share her home island experiences. The island songs all had a happy reggae beat, and since knowing Huzzy the girls had all learned more than a few of these tunes.

Now Huzzy sang her lizard song as they filled the water jug again and headed back to their camp. Her island accent filled the groves with a happy sound.

> *A girl she pick a flower*
> *To bring her mama fair.*
> *The girl she do not see*
> *The lizard that be there.*
> *Her mama see the lizard*
> *So tiny and so green*
> *She say, "Thank you, my daughter,*
> *It is the best I have seen."*
> *The girl be so surprised*
> *When her mama throw away*
> *The flower that she pick*
> *And she let the lizard stay!*

The words of the jolly song even made Libby laugh, and she thought Huzzy might be right. Now if she saw another lizard she would think of the mama in the song keeping the lizard and throwing away the flower on which it came. When they were back at the camp, Sarah put water on to boil and kept the rest on a shelf made from boxes that once held food supplies from the *Sea Breeze*. While the breakfast of fresh conch and cut-up plums, figs, and wild cherries was being made, Allison, Annie, and Libby watched as Shawn worked on grinding and mashing more of the things she and Annie had collected. As usual, Shawn sat apart from the others, but the results of her experiments were so interesting that even Allison couldn't resist watching.

"So many colours!" Annie exclaimed, looking at the big brown leaf that now had stripes of bright yellow, orange, purple, white, red, and even a lavender-blue.

"It's like the best make-up counter at the shops," Allison marvelled.

Usually when Allison said something like that, Shawn had no patience for it. But this time it gave Shawn an idea. "Would you like to try some of it on?" she asked Allison.

Allison, who had been without make-up for longer than she ever thought possible, couldn't hide her excitement. "Try it," she said. Then she sat down in front of Shawn's leaf palette and let Shawn paint her face. The artist chose a dab of the lavender-blue to put on Allison's eyelids. It made her green eyes snap to life. Then she painted Allison's lips with a plum colour, but she wasn't finished. On Allison's left cheek, Shawn painted a bright orange sun. On her right cheek she painted a pale white moon.

"Oh, I love it, Shawn!" Annie cried. "Will you do me next?"

"Then me," Libby pleaded.

Shawn painted a rainbow on Annie's cheek and a plum-coloured heart on Libby's cheek. Sarah stopped cooking long enough to have a cluster of yellow stars sprinkled over her nose and cheeks, and even Huzzy bent down for a tiny sailing boat to be painted on her cheek. The only one without a decoration was herself. So looking in Allison's mirror, Shawn painted a small yellow-and-white flower on her own left cheekbone.

The six painted girls were all in a happy mood as they ate the food they had almost grown used to. The paint gave them a fresh start that they needed after all the events of the day before. Bad moods seemed painted over, and the pretty face decorations led to more painting. After the breakfast dishes were cleaned, arms, legs, fingernails, toes, and even hair were given a new look with painted zigzags, polka dots, stripes, swirls, and simple brush strokes. Huzzy had intended to get an early start on the boat, but for the first time in a long while the girls seemed to actually be having fun. For the moment none of them was thinking about danger or missing home. Libby, for once, didn't have a mind full of frightening visions. Allison was happy just to be wearing eyeshadow again. And they had all finally found a way to get Shawn to be a part of the group. Her attachment to the island separated her from all the others who only wanted to leave it.

Huzzy watched her girls sitting still for paint, then as one was finished another came back for more. Under the paint they got into the spirit of play and danced around the beach as they sang Huzzy's lizard song. The scene was the happiest Huzzy had witnessed in all their days here. Her feeling of urgency about leaving the island was calmed for the moment, and she didn't mention the building of the boat again that day. Instead she just let them have the freedom to laugh and run in and out of the water.

"Come and swim with us, Huzzy!" Annie called out happily.

"It's warm as toast," Sarah assured her, splashing a little water Huzzy's way.

"Why did you have to mention toast?" Allison said, being careful not to get her face wet. Already the paint on their arms and legs was washing off, leaving only faded stains where it had been.

Huzzy didn't need convincing. She cast her worries aside and ran into the water to join the others. "Come, Shawn!" she shouted to the last girl. "Come and show us how to really swim."

Shawn was the swimmer in the group. She never stuck a toe in first to test the water. She was never content to just sit at the water's edge and splash. Her way was to just run in and keep swimming out to sea. At Huzzy's invitation, Shawn put down her paints and brushes and came running in. She passed the splashers and kept going and going, all the way to where the water changed from clear turquoise to deep purple. She was out by the reefs, farther than any of them had ever dared to go.

Libby hated to see Shawn go out so far. Her happy, carefree mind suddenly clouded over as one of her pictures began forming in her head. She couldn't see clearly what the danger was, but in her mind she saw Shawn swimming too far out and the water coming back to shore without her. Before the picture was finished, Shawn had already turned around and was coming back. When the girl came running safely out of the water again, shaking the water off and looking like a joyful mermaid emerging from a friendly sea, Libby scolded herself for letting her own fears spoil a good mood.

"You go out too far," Libby couldn't help saying.

"What's too far?" Shawn asked, tilting her face up to the sun to dry it. "It's wonderful out there. The water's colder, the fish are more colourful, and the coral fans are much more beautiful."

"It is true," Huzzy agreed. "The farther out one swims, the more beautiful the sights. Only be sure you see everything before it sees you."

Shawn laughed. "I'm not afraid of fish and coral," she said. "And the colours are hard to resist."

"Speaking of colours," Annie said, examining her toes and seeing that the paint had been washed away. "Will you paint me again?"

"Me, too," Libby said, glad to get her mind back to happier things.

So the rest of the day was given to painting and swimming and painting again. By the time the sun started turning the sky orange, then pink, then lavender the girls should have been tired out. Instead, the day of fun and togetherness gave them a new burst of energy. Before supper they all followed Shawn to her shelter for the addition of a shell to the counting wall. It was always a beautiful moment when Shawn solemnly lifted the new conch shell up to the sky and whispered the number of the shell before she placed it alongside the one from the day before.

"One hundred and seventeen days," Shawn said softly. "One hundred and seventeen days at home on our island," she said almost to herself.

The others didn't say anything when Shawn said this. By now they knew her feelings. To them the shells counted the days away from home. And even though they all shared in the ritual, the wall belonged to Shawn.

Once the shell was added, the girls were more than ready for supper. The swimming and running all day had given them all good appetites. "I'll be there in a few minutes," Shawn called after them as the other five headed back to the camp down the beach. While the scene was still fresh in her mind, Shawn wanted to quickly draw a picture of the girls in their painted faces looking as happy as she was on the island. As usual, she started to leave herself out of the picture, but just this once she included a figure that was her own.

It wasn't because she had joined them, she thought to herself. It was because for the first time it seemed that they had joined her. She finished a quick sketch on the back of another sketch that was on paper, and put it on the pile of drawings that told the whole story from the very first day of this adventure. Then, Shawn walked out of the clearing and took the long way to the main camp. She walked by the water. The sunset was the most beautiful she'd ever seen, and she wanted to be as close to it as she could. As she watched the colours change as dramatically as in a kaleidoscope, she breathed in the island air and loved it more than ever. With her eyes to the sky, she walked at the water's edge not seeing the sand beneath her feet. When her toe hit something solid she looked down, and what she saw was a complete surprise. It was an orange. But it couldn't be. Not here on the island. There were no orange trees. She picked it up and turned it over in her hand. It was round and firm. "Fresh," Shawn said aloud.

She looked ahead a little to see if there were more. To her surprise, there were several more oranges, and floating in with the tide were a few lemons and a lime. Shawn looked out at the horizon to see where the fruits might be coming from. She saw nothing but a flock of gulls swooping down to find fish for supper. As quickly as she could, she gathered the fruits in her arms and checked to see that none had escaped her. Her heart was beating fast because a certain reality hit her. She knew the oranges, and lemons, and lime could only have come from a boat or a ship passing by somewhere out of their sight. The waters near the island were too shallow for any boats to sail, but out there, beyond the reefs, beyond the edge of the channel, ships did go by. One of those ships had dropped something, and Shawn was secretly thankful that she was the one who had found them.

With her arms loaded, she quickly looked up the beach towards the camp. She was close enough to see the figures of the girls moving about getting things ready for supper. She hoped they couldn't see her. Without thinking twice about whether or not what she was going to do was right or wrong, Shawn turned back in the direction of her shelter and began to run. When she got there, she hurried along the path behind her tent, following the same route she and Annie had taken the day before. It was an easy walk this time because she knew the way. She was out of breath when she got where she wanted to be. With her chest heaving and her heart pounding, Shawn threw the oranges, the lemons, and the lime one by one into the sinkhole that had tried to take Annie before. She stood there in the dusky light and watched as each fruit was gulped down with a satisfied *glub*.

When the last fruit had been swallowed, Shawn breathed easier and took her time walking back. Now she had the time to think about what she'd just done. She'd found evidence of people out there on that ocean and had made the decision to hide it. Was it so wrong? she wondered. Everyone had had so much fun on the island all day. Shawn thought maybe they were finally going to start seeing it the way she saw it, as a beautiful paradise. Why spoil the change in feeling by getting their hopes up about some ship that passed too far from them anyway?

The fruits were gone, but her hands still held their aroma. A sweet mixture of citrus juices bathed her hands and soaked into the pores. The smell stayed no matter how much she rubbed her hands on the palmetto leaves. She crushed plums in her palms until her hands were purple, and she hoped the heavier smell of them covered the lighter citrus smell.

When Shawn came running up to the camp with her purple hands the others noticed right away. "What's on your hands?" Annie asked.

"Stains," Shawn answered. "I was making more paint from plums."

Always the mother, Sarah looked at the stains, shook her head and said, "What you really need to get those stains out is some fresh lemon juice."

Shawn didn't say a word.

4
Hope

Shawn was sorry. She really was. It was too late to
get the sunken fruits back to show the others, and
she wasn't sure how to tell Huzzy about finding
them without explaining what she had done with
them. The stains on her hands made her feel
ashamed of what she'd done, but she would find a
way to make it right. She made up her mind that
she would do two things to make up for her bad
deed: She would finish the boat picture, and she
would work extra hard to get the rudder board as
smooth as Huzzy said it needed to be. Once she
had done things to show Huzzy that she was trying
to help, she knew Huzzy would forgive her. Well,
she hoped she would, anyway. With these thoughts
in her mind, Shawn quickly got up, looked down
the beach to the camp, and saw that the others
were not stirring yet. Only Huzzy seemed to be
busy doing something over by the rocks. In the
pale light of early dawn, Shawn started painting
the boat.

As the sun climbed higher, burning off the morning mist, the other girls woke up without nudging from Huzzy. They all seemed willing workers after their fun the day before. Even Allison was up with the sun and ready to dig her hands into the mud pots again.

Sarah made breakfast while Annie and Libby walked over to see what Huzzy was doing there by the rocks. "Morning, Huzzy," Annie said to the tall girl bent double over a pile of shells on a flat rock.

"Good morning!' she greeted Annie and Libby. She stood up, and the girls could see she'd been grinding and crushing shells that would make the mud mixture dry to a water-resistant cement in the boat's cracks. "It is good you are up early today. I have been looking at our boat, and I believe if we stay with her through the day we shall be able to finish."

"Finish?" Libby squealed excitedly. "Really? Finish?"

Huzzy laughed as she always did when the red-haired girl bubbled over like lemonade from a bottle that's been shaken. "Yes, I did some rubbing last night on the rudder board. Another day in Shawn's hands might finish that. We shall see how far we get today before the sun stops us."

"Breakfast!" Sarah called out cheerfully.

Annie did a double take. For a second her sister

sounded just like their mother. It wouldn't have surprised Annie a bit if her father had come whistling up the beach ready to throw an arm around each of his daughters and walk them in to the breakfast room in their Florida house.

"Come and get it!" Sarah called out in her mother's voice again.

"Huzzy," Annie said softly, "do you really think we might finish today? And does that mean we'll be going . . ."

"Home?" Libby finished.

Huzzy thought of the boat and then answered truthfully. "That is our hope," she said.

Allison's voice came squawking through the air. "You lot," she yelled, "are you going to eat, or what?"

Huzzy, Libby, and Annie all answered the call by running through the sand to the table area where Sarah had set out bowls of fruit and plates of fried fish. The table was set for six, but Shawn was not yet there.

Huzzy looked up the beach and tried to see the sixth girl. At first she didn't see any sign of her slender figure moving around her shelter area. Then Shawn stepped out of her tent and stood looking towards the ocean. She felt eyes watching her and turned her head in Huzzy's direction. Shawn waved and then ran through the sand, straight into the bright turquoise-blue water. As she did every morning, Shawn swam a long way out doing dolphin dives all the way. No distance was too much for her good, strong stroke.

While the other girls started eating their breakfast, Huzzy kept her eye on Shawn who was still swimming out. When she had got so far that her head was only a dot in Huzzy's eye, Shawn did another dive and turned back towards shore. Her tanned arms reached forwards and pulled her closer and closer. She moved through the water like a fast fish, and she did not see what Huzzy thought *she* saw suddenly coming up behind Shawn.

Huzzy blinked her eyes to clear them and looked harder at what could only be a grey fin. The shape of it was unmistakable even from a distance.

"Shark!" shouted Huzzy in a voice none of the girls had heard before. The word boomed through the air in Shawn's direction but didn't reach her. "Shark!" Huzzy bellowed again.

The other girls, who hadn't been watching Shawn at all, were shocked to see Huzzy's long black legs leaping through the air as she ran down the beach shouting all the way. They all followed as fast as they could and added their own shouts of "Shark!" to Huzzy's.

Shawn's stroke continued to bring her in, but the fin followed closer and closer as though it were somehow connected to the swimmer. She still had no idea that she was being shadowed by a shark, so panic did not slow her down or take her concentration away.

The others caught up to Huzzy in time to see Shawn stepping through the water towards the beach, wringing her hair out in her hands, and at last seeing and hearing Huzzy. "What?" Shawn said in a startled voice. She heard the word *shark* and instinctively turned around to look where she'd been. The grey fin was a body-length away, but had turned out to sea again. It was too shallow for the sharp-toothed shark, and it had no choice but to give up.

Huzzy grabbed Shawn and pulled her the rest of the way out. Then she threw her arms around her and held onto the dripping wet girl as though it were a final goodbye rather than a grateful hello. Annie added her own arms to the hug, but Libby stood frozen to the spot where she stood. She watched the place where the fin had been but was no more. Her head filled with terrible pictures that were clearer than the ones in her mind the day before. She saw a shark's mouth open and aiming for Shawn's kicking feet. She saw teeth tearing skin. Her eyes closed. When she opened them again and looked at the water, it looked innocent.

Sarah stood holding a towel out for Shawn. "Here," she said, when the hugging circle broke up. "Oh, Shawn, you're all right, thank goodness." She put the towel around Shawn's shoulders.

"I am all right, really," Shawn said. "I didn't even see it. I think you all had the worst of it because you knew it was there."

"It is true," Huzzy agreed. "What you do not know about makes no difference to you."

"And it's gone now," Shawn said, looking back at the sea. She pulled the towel around her shoulders and thought how lucky she was to have got ashore safely. The island likes me best, the voice in her head said again. But the calmness she showed at first turned into a shivering that she couldn't control. It wasn't a shiver from cold; it was from a mixture of fear and relief.

Huzzy saw Shawn's body reacting to the narrow escape, and her own body shivered quickly. Inside her chest her heart beat too fast. Anxiety gripped her, forcing her to remember the feeling she'd had the day before. It was urgent that she get the girls off the island. In all the weeks and months on the island no one had stepped into a sinkhole. Until now. No one had been slashed by the blades of the bayonet plant. Until now. No one had been threatened by a hungry grey-finned hunter. Until now. It was time to leave.

"The boat," Huzzy said. "We must finish the boat. Nothing must stop us now."

None of the girls questioned Huzzy's serious

statement. They could feel the change in her mood. Her usual serenity was replaced by a sense of watchfulness. Like a runner in sprint position at the starting line of a race, Huzzy seemed ready to take off, and the others caught the feeling.

"I'm all right," Shawn said again. "Really." She could see that Huzzy had her mind on one thing, finishing the boat, and all of the girls had seen Huzzy's determination before. Anything she set her mind to, she accomplished. Shawn had no doubt in her mind. The boat would be finished today.

They were all just as glad to leave the place where Shawn had been shadowed by the shark. Now there was one more spot on the island that held a memory of a dangerous encounter. Huzzy didn't sing any of her cheerful island songs on the way to the cove where the boat waited.

Allison, Sarah, and Libby walked together, followed by Shawn and Annie. The mood was quiet, but the blue sky and warm breeze helped to lift their spirits as they followed Huzzy up the purple, cratered rocks. The six of them stood above the cove and faced the task at hand. Even after a day away from it, the boat didn't look any better to their eyes. It was still a heavy, hulking, ugly bulge that stood out like a wart on the smooth white sand. The tide was low, which made the boat seem impossibly far from its goal, the water.

"Oh, thank goodness," Libby breathed. "Low tide."

"But look at all the sand crabs!" Annie gasped as she saw whole patches of beach moving sideways as the little crabs did a chorus line walk, first to one side then to the other. "I love how that looks from up here, but I'm glad they bury themselves in the sand when we get close."

Shawn looked at the water with a new respect after swimming with the shark. She didn't see any more fins, but Huzzy's earlier words came back to her: "What you do not know about makes no difference to you." The problem was, now she *did* know about sharks. She hated the fear she now felt towards the ocean she loved so much. The boat, which would carry them safely over the water, looked better to her than it had before her morning swim.

"Well, what are we all standing around up here for?" Allison asked impatiently.

"Can't wait to get your hands in the mud again?" Annie sniggered.

"Can't wait to finish this work and finally see if it will really float," Allison threw back. "I hate to think what it's going to be like if it won't do what it's supposed to do."

"I do not think you have to worry about that," Huzzy said confidently. "We have followed the methods of the old boat builders years ago before the time of power tools. She may not be pretty, but I do believe she will stay afloat in the water.''

Sarah looked into the boat and had a clear view of Huzzy's handiwork at the bow. There were shelves hollowed out of logs. These were for the supplies they would carry. Food, of course, would be the main cargo. Most of the room in the boat would be for the girls. The *Sea Breeze*, which had seemed close-quartered when the girls first went on board, now in Sarah's memory became tremendous compared to the cramped homemade boat. There would be no place for suitcases or any of the shell collections, plaited rope rugs, or driftwood sculptures made on lazy afternoons, or even Shawn's paintings. Just the girls, the food, and as much fresh water as they could carry. Sarah breathed an anxious sigh, lifted her head high, and was the first to follow Huzzy down to the floor of the cove.

For the rest of the warm morning, the girls worked hard at their jobs, and Huzzy checked the work even more closely. Shawn rubbed the rudder board until her arms ached, but at last it passed Huzzy's inspection. When the sun was directly above them and heat began to bear down, making their skin feel hot and dry, Huzzy stopped the work. "But today we will come back to it after the sun has moved over a bit. We are too close now to leave it.'' Her eyes focused on the boat, and she cocked her head to one side to catch every angle.

The tide was crawling up, sending the sand crabs scurrying. When the water fell back, the daring crabs poked their heads out of the sand holes to see if the coast was clear. Water scared them back into the sand again, and sent them digging their way to spots where water wasn't yet. The girls left them to their survival game and went back to the camp for lunch. No one really felt like going for a swim even though they were hot enough. The memory of the fin was too fresh in their minds, and it seemed safer to just sit under the cool fan leaves of the ferns and wait for the sun to slip lower in the sky.

Huzzy took the opportunity to speak to them all about something important. "My girls," she began quietly, "it does not seem so long ago that I stood before you holding the board from the *Sea Breeze* and said that we would begin to build a boat."

"Ha," Allison couldn't help saying. "It seems long ago to *me*!"

"Hush!" Sarah said. "Let Huzzy talk."

"Sorry," said Allison, holding her long hair up off her neck.

"Well, I do not mean it has not been *too* long to be away from our homes, but we have all worked very hard and I believe today is the day our work will be done." She hesitated as the girls all talked at once excitedly.

"Finally! Can you believe it? Finished!" they said amidst hugs and dancing around. Even Allison threw a careless arm around Sarah, forgetting for a moment that for the past months Sarah's constant mothering of all of them had driven her crazy.

"It is happy news." Huzzy smiled proudly. "And when the tide is just right it will be time to test our work."

"You mean, put the boat in the water?" Annie said, her eyes widening.

"But not us in it yet, you don't mean?" Libby asked, fearing that it might not float.

Huzzy knew what she had to say would be frightening to them, so she chose her words carefully. "I have thought a great deal about *how* we must do what we must do," she said slowly. "The tide will only help us once. That is to say, it will help us pull the boat out, but once we have her in the water we will not be able to bring her back into the cove."

"Then how do we test it?" Libby wondered. Her throat tightened as she spoke. She was afraid she already knew the answer. Sarah put an arm around Libby as Huzzy answered her question.

"We must first load her up with the food supplies we will take and whatever else we can manage to fit in. Then I will take her out through the hard currents of the riptide."

"No, Huzzy!" Sarah said. "You can't go alone!"

"What if the boat sinks?" Libby worried.

"I will swim to shore," Huzzy said calmly.

"But what if it just goes without us?" Allison asked more selfishly.

"It will not," replied Huzzy.

"But what if — " Annie began.

Huzzy held up a hand to stop the questions. "I will take her through the tide, and if she sails the way she will need to sail to get us away from Chilas Cay to one of the other islands where people are living, I will sail her around the cove reef to the calmer waters on the other side."

"And pick us all up, you mean?" Annie asked.

"Yes, exactly," said Huzzy.

"It's too dangerous for you, though," Sarah insisted.

"But I must do this, Sarah. It is the only way." Huzzy appreciated Sarah's concern, but she knew there was no other choice.

Shawn, who had not said anything all morning moved next to Huzzy, looked at her with her yellow-brown eyes, and spoke. "Let me go with you, Huzzy. I'm not afraid, and you'll need help getting the boat around the reef. What if the mast doesn't hold the sail when the wind fills it? What if the rudder snaps again? You'll need someone with you. Let me go, too."

The silent bond that existed between the two girls who looked so different, yet were so similar inside was evident to the others as their eyes stayed fixed on each others' for a moment. Huzzy was thinking. Then she reached out and placed one hand on Shawn's shoulder. "As you wish," Huzzy said. "We shall go together."

It was a serious moment until Allison spoke. "Well, just make sure you two don't take the best seats on the boat!" She said it with a straight face, but couldn't hold it for long. All the girls had to laugh. There were no seats in the boat. There was no best spot, either. It was all going to be bumpy and rough, but the girls who once might have complained would be grateful if only the boat would take them back to civilization.

The laughter took some of the tension away as they went back to the cove to work together in pulling up the big mast pole that had been rescued from the *Sea Breeze*. In the storm the whole mast had fallen and landed on Huzzy's ankle, giving her a bad sprain that lasted for weeks. The bad ankle caused a lot of inconvenience at the time, but the fallen mast had been easy to remove from the boat before it dipped slowly into the sea. Now that same mast was going to have another chance at holding a sail out for the wind to fill.

A log had been hollowed out for the base of the mast to fit into. It was a tight fit, and that was just how Huzzy wanted it. All the lines were in place, and there was an extra rope tied to it so that four girls could pull while the other two pushed the long pole up until it stood straight about two thirds of the way to the bow of the boat.

Even though the sun wasn't beating down as strongly as it did at noon, it was still hot and hard work for the girls. Huzzy and Shawn pushed. The others pulled. Just as the mast was about to be completely raised, Annie and Libby let the rope slide through their hands by mistake.

"Annie!" shouted Sarah. "Hold on!"

"I can't!" she shouted back. "It's burning my hands."

"Mine, too!" Libby yelled as the splintery rope slipped too quickly through her small fingers.

Sarah saved the mast by reaching around the two smaller girls and pulling extra hard to stop the rope from running out. Huzzy and Shawn helped by pushing extra hard on the mast to give Sarah more slack in the rope. One more hard pull from Sarah and one more push from Shawn and Huzzy and the mast was up. Huzzy hurried to hammer in the nails at the base to hold it in place. Then she wrapped the rope around and around until the mast looked solidly anchored into the deck.

With sweat dripping down their faces and their hands red and sore, the girls stood back from the boat and for the first time they thought it looked like one. The mast was just what it needed to change it from almost a boat to *really* a boat.

"Hooray!" bubbled Libby, forgetting her sore hands. "It looks great!"

"Beautiful." Sarah smiled, feeling proud of the work.

"Well, *now* there's hope," Allison said.

"Yes," said Huzzy, putting a hand on each hip. She looked at the boat and had to agree with Allison. "*There* is hope."

5
Oceans of Night

The boat had taken months to build. Morning after morning after morning the girls had worked towards the day when at last Huzzy would say, "My girls, our work is done." Days had gone by slowly, but now the time to leave the island seemed suddenly to have arrived. As if without warning, the girls felt hurried when they had to carefully choose only the most essential things to bring with them on the journey that might take them no further than the cove's currents, or all the way to Huzzy's Green Turtle Cay. Decisions were difficult.

No one had really thought about what would be left behind. Except Shawn. She had thought of everything that would be left, and she didn't want to leave any of it. Even her near brush with the shark didn't make her in a hurry to forsake her beautiful island.

For Allison, packing to leave the island was just

as difficult as packing for the cruise had been. She stood looking over clothes that were now faded and stiff from saltwater washings. The truth of the matter was none of them was too great. She could almost hear her mother's voice in her ear. "Allison, you don't really think you're going to bring *that* with you, do you?" Then her mother would have pushed her aside and taken over the packing just as she'd done before. Now that Allison was on her own and left to pack for herself, she tried to be sensible, for once. She chose only the warm clothes and one cooler pair of shorts and a T-shirt. The make-up case, now full of empty bottles and compacts, wouldn't be coming on this boat. Neither would the fancy shoes that hadn't been worn yet nor the dresses that matched them. Wouldn't her mother have a fit if she saw Allison leaving out the best things of all!

Sarah, Annie, and Libby were more naturally sensible and had no trouble picking clothes. For them it was more difficult leaving the small things they'd collected or made in their months there. Huzzy organized a small pile that included the toolbox from the *Sea Breeze* and the nautical charts that showed all the Abaco Islands except the tiny one on which six girls were stranded.

When the rest had finished choosing and rejecting things, Shawn had still not begun. Although she had left home carrying the least amount of luggage, she had accumulated the most things while on the island. Her shelter was more permanent than just a sleeping mat and was filled with homely things she'd made for comfort. It was very hard to think of leaving her tent with its painted walls and the humming-birds who liked to flutter by on their way to the plum tree blossoms. Then there was the counting wall, which had grown in length and in meaning. Each shell represented another event and another day spent in an adventure in paradise. Hardest of all for Shawn was the realization that her paintings and drawings would have to stay behind. The piles of papers and painted stones, shells, and tree bark were everywhere in the tent. There wasn't a special moment that Shawn hadn't recorded in her work. To leave it behind would be like leaving a diary or family album somewhere where it would never be seen again. She knew that once they were off the island they would never come back.

In spite of the fact that it would not go with her, Shawn wanted to finish her painting of the boat. She spent the next couple of hours making her paints from the leaves, flowers, and fruits she and Annie had collected, and then worked until the painting was finished. She hadn't noticed that the afternoon had slowly slipped away and was surprised when the other girls arrived for the counting wall ritual.

"You finished it!" Annie said excitedly.

"On the same day we all finished it," Sarah added. "It's beautiful, Shawn."

"It is," Huzzy said solemnly. "I am sorry, Shawn. So sorry, really." The others didn't know what Huzzy meant at first, but Shawn did.

"I knew I wouldn't be able to take it, but I wanted to finish it, anyway. Who knows? Maybe another storm will bring another boat with another group." Shawn smiled and held back tears.

"And maybe they'll like art!" Libby said, trying to be cheerful, but it didn't really help.

The girls looked around at the piles of drawings and paintings that Shawn had been sorting through and suddenly realized Shawn's pain. No one had anything to say that would make her feel better, and Shawn's sadness started to spread over all of them.

Even Allison, who had never thought much of Shawn, had to admit her work was good. No, great. "I can't believe you really did all of these," she said with new admiration in her voice.

"Did you think I only painted faces?" Shawn asked, half kidding.

Allison answered seriously. "No. I suppose painting my own face with make-up is the only thing *I've* ever painted, that's all. But you really have a talent. You're lucky."

"Thank you," Shawn said. In all the time they'd

been together these were the first kind words they'd exchanged.

"Shall we do the shell now?" Huzzy interrupted. She was eager to load the things onto the boat so that they could catch the early morning high tide.

Shawn had the next shell ready. It was the biggest one so far, a queen conch with a yellowish-buff colour outside and a beautiful rose-pink inside. She carefully picked up the shell and faced the ocean as she always did. Under the sky that matched the inside of the shell, the ocean looked more beautiful than it had ever looked before. Fading sunlight bounced off the rippling surface like spilled pearls, and the colours that changed because of the coral reefs below were deeper and more purple than the darkest vineyard grapes. The warm island breeze blew through all the girls' long hair, caressing them as a mother's hand might.

Shawn began to speak, "One hundred and . . ." But she couldn't continue. She couldn't bring herself to say the number that would be the last night on Chilas Cay. She couldn't even hold the shell that would symbolize the completion of the counting wall. The queen conch shell fell from her hands and somehow landed right where it was supposed to.

"One hundred and eighteen, I believe it is," Huzzy said. "And this shell, the biggest shell of all, must stand for our biggest accomplishment. The boat."

"The boat," they all said together like an "Amen" at the end of a prayer.

Huzzy put an arm around Shawn as a way of encouraging her to finish her packing. "You know, Shawn," she said, "you may leave your work behind you, but you take your talent with you. Some people leave a place with nothing. That will never happen to you, yes?"

As so often happened, Huzzy's wise words got another girl through another rough moment. Shawn filled a small rucksack with only the few items of clothing she absolutely needed. The rest would stay behind. Without looking back, she followed Huzzy and the others back to the camp where they ate a quick supper of the usual fish and fruit. Then with a mixture of sadness, joy, and excitement, the girls made the several trips back and forth from the camp to the boat, carrying supplies and their few personal belongings. As she had done on the *Sea Breeze*, Huzzy organized all the cargo and assigned places inside the boat.

"Tomorrow," explained Huzzy, "we must wake up very, very early. The tide will be waiting for us, but not for long. Now the boat is ready to do her job for us. And we must be ready, too."

An orange ball of a sun sat sinking on the horizon. The girls stood in a close group listening to Huzzy's instructions for the morning. They were all quite sure they would have no trouble getting up early.

"I don't think I'll sleep at all tonight," Libby said. "I'm too excited." The water in the cove lurked at the edges of the rocky walls and was on the way out. Libby was glad to see it go. Her feet never felt free to walk on this side of the wall. She hated it because that tide always seemed to be reaching for her. The whole time she worked inside the boat she heard the water pounding, as if knocking before it came to get her. "No," Libby said again. "I don't think I'll sleep at all."

"Me, neither," Annie said.

"Well, I think this is one night we won't really need the home fires," Allison said.

"Oh," said Sarah in the voice that always reminded Annie of Wendy in *Peter Pan*, "let's have the fires as usual. If this is the last night, we should light the fires as a celebration at least."

A sudden swifter breeze sent a quick ripple over the water. The wind sent shivers through the bare-shouldered girls, and they huddled even closer to hear the rest of Huzzy's words.

Huzzy looked to the direction of the wind and remembered how a wind like this made her mother get up and pull the wooden shutters closed on the windows of their pink stucco house with the jumbay trees outside the door. She said what her

Mama Selina might have said if she'd been standing on a beach at sunset with a cooler wind coming. "Hurry now, my girls. Back to the camp. There is no sense in letting the wind chill us to the bone. Let us go back and leave the wind alone."

With teeth chattering a little, the girls again climbed up and over the wall and ran through the still-warm sand back to their camp. It didn't look the same now that some things had been moved onto the boat. The kitchen area, especially, seemed bare. Everything except what they needed for one more night and an early breakfast had been removed. It reminded Sarah of her family's summerhouse on the first day they arrived every summer. It was empty, just waiting to be lived in again. The camp had the same look, except, thought Sarah, it won't ever be lived in once we're gone. The new wind blowing through the palmetto leaves made her think of curtains in an empty cottage blowing out of the open windows. She felt surprised by a feeling of sorrow, not for herself or the other girls, but for the island that would be left alone again. Before they had come to it no one was known to have been on Chilas Cay except the captain for whom the island was named more than two hundred years ago. Would it be another two hundred years before other human voices would be heard here?

Sarah knew she was probably being too dramatic

in thinking the island had feelings. The only feelings she had to worry about were her own and the other girls'. For so many days and nights they had been like her family. She'd played her game of being the mother in *Swiss Family Robinson* and then switched to Wendy in *Peter Pan*. Both roles were easy for her to fill, and her lost girls had counted on her to comfort them, cook for them, care for them just like a real mother. She thought about the boat and the possible dangers they would face once they were in it. Her own fears had to be pushed away. She had to be strong and brave for the others. That's what they would expect from her, and that's what she would give them.

Libby and Annie were both happy to be tucked in by Sarah that night. They were too excited to sleep, but the wind blew chilly and the cover felt good. "Sarah?" Annie said when her sister pulled the blanket up for her.

"What is it, Anniekins?" Sarah answered softly.

"Are you afraid?" Annie sat up and leaned on one elbow waiting for the answer. Libby listened, too.

"A little," Sarah admitted. "Are you?"

"A little," said Annie.

"A *lot*," Libby added. Even lying on her mat she could almost feel the rocking she was sure they'd feel in the big, bulky boat. Her mind flipped from one terrible picture to another, as if it were changing channels on a television. First she saw that threatening tide pulling her away from the girls and not releasing her no matter how hard she fought. Then she saw sharks circling, looking hungry and eager for the waves to drop her from their grip. Then she saw the face of her dear aunt Alice, weeping as she walked through the lonely rooms of the house they used to share before Libby was lost.

Allison did her job with the fires. "It's a good thing we'll be leaving," she said as she lit the last fire. "The matches are finally about gone." She stirred the dried sticks around with a longer stick and then settled down on her mat and watched the flames suddenly catch and reach skyward, sending a long shadowy arm over the backs of the other three girls who lay on their stomachs watching the fire, too.

Shawn, of course, chose to spend her last night in her own shelter. The wind blowing stronger through her tent didn't chill her. But the knowledge that this would be her final night on the island sent a sorry shiver through her. In the darkness she made a silent promise to herself that some day, somehow she would come back to this place. *If* they got away from it safely, she thought.

Huzzy was as excited as the others. She truly didn't think she would sleep a wink, even though it would be better if she got plenty of rest. She thought of the task ahead of her in the morning.

That tide was fierce, and she knew she would have only one chance to get the boat out. If she lost her hold on it, the tide could take *her* from them. It was with these thoughts in her mind that she lay listening to Sarah, Annie, and Libby talking quietly. Every once in a while Allison added something. Eventually, as the home fires settled down, so did the girls. Soon, even Huzzy's eyes couldn't fight the sleep that sneaked up on her in the darkness. It was their last night on the island, and although none of them thought they would sleep, all of the girls slept so soundly they didn't notice the wind picking up.

Libby felt it first and wasn't sure if it was real or in her dreams. She opened her eyes cautiously and looked out into the night. In darkness familiar things disappear and strange things take their places. Monster shapes crawl in and stand where trees stood in daylight. Whispers that were evening breezes are chased away by haunting howls of ghosts. Sand turns to quicksand. Waves turn tidal. And daydreams turn to nightmares stubborn to stay until darkness turns to daylight again. Libby saw nothing that looked familiar, and then she was sure she must be dreaming with open eyes. The others were asleep, and she felt completely alone with the strangers of the night. She began to whimper quietly, not wanting to wake anyone but secretly wishing one of the others would wake up and keep her company.

"What is it, Libby?" Sarah's concerned but sleepy voice whispered. She reached her arm out to Libby and rested it across her back where the home fire's shadow had held her earlier. "Are you dreaming again?"

"No, I don't think so," Libby whispered back. "Something feels different, doesn't it? The air. Is it the air?"

Both girls looked out at the ocean and could not see where the night left off and the ocean began. The air was warm and cold at once, and it swirled around them, lifting the corners of their mats and covers. The tall casuarina trees that always leaned to the northwest were blown to the northeast and their branches rustled like petticoats on a dance floor.

"Girls," came Huzzy's hushed voice right next to Sarah's ear, making Sarah jump. "I am sorry to startle you, but we must all get up. It is a storm coming. We must hurry to the cove. It will take all our strength if we are to save the boat."

Libby and Sarah could hardly believe what they were hearing. "Save the boat?" What did she mean? But they obeyed quickly. Sarah shook Annie awake, and Libby went over to Allison and got her up.

"What's going on?" Allison wanted to know, but the wind was stronger now, and she could feel that a storm was on the way even though the darkness didn't let her see it.

"Storm!" Huzzy answered anyway. "We must go to the cove!"

"But it's too dark!" Libby shouted out through the pitch-black.

"We must go. We must, Libby. Stay close to me if you are frightened." Huzzy held out a hand but was already heading towards the beach.

"Huzzy!" Shawn's voice called out. She came running from her place to warn the others of what they already knew. "A storm! The boat!" The same wind that woke Libby had blown across Shawn's tent, causing the sailcloth to make a *thwapping* sound that snapped her awake, too. Afraid that she might be the only one awake, she ran into the wind and reached the camp breathless.

"Hurry, girls," Huzzy called out over the sound that was beginning to roar in their ears. They'd all heard the sound before. It was the same sound that had pounded in their ears the day the *Sea Breeze* was wrecked by another storm.

The girls held hands and made a train as they followed Huzzy in the direction of the cove. Without warning, the sky dumped buckets of hard rain down on them. The wind tried to hold them back, and the rain slapped against their faces, but Huzzy kept pulling Libby, who pulled Sarah, Annie, Allison, and Shawn along. The rocky wall was hard enough to climb in daylight when time allowed for slow and careful steps. In the dark, with wind and rain acting as guards for the cove, it was almost impossible to get over the wall. Huzzy struggled and kept going until she heard a scream behind her.

"Libby!" Huzzy called back, trying to see what had happened at the other end of the hand she held.

"My foot is caught!" Libby shouted back.

"I've got it." Sarah's voice came over the hissing rains and thundering gale winds. Sarah felt down Libby's leg until she found the foot that was lodged between two sharp points of rock. Libby had on trainers that were worn and torn even before this trouble. Now she was forced to leave the trapped shoe behind and go on with one foot bare.

Huzzy waited but leaned into the wind so she wouldn't be knocked off the top of the wall. If she fell they'd all fall. Her eyes searched the cove for the outline of the boat, but it was too dark to see. The noise of the waves crashing on the rocks and against each other sounded like the bombs of war, and Huzzy hoped she and the girls would not be the losers. "Come, girls!" she shouted. "I cannot see her, but let us hope she is still there! We must push her back from the tide!"

Libby was terrified. The tide that was always

after her seemed to be bellowing her name with the crash of every wave. She could not see it, but all around her she felt its presence. Her tears fell as hard and fast as the rain, but still Huzzy pulled her down, down to the cove. There was no turning back because the others were behind her. She was trapped, but at last her one bare foot felt wet sand instead of rock. They were in the cove.

"The boat!" Huzzy's voice cried out over the booming noises. She let go of Libby's hand, causing Libby to scream in terror at being left. But Huzzy had to leave her to save the boat. "Help me!" she yelled as she stood in front of the boat. The others tried to follow her voice since their eyes were useless in the darkness. They all felt the water around their legs, but Huzzy's cry for help was more desperate than their need to avoid the water.

All of them leaned against the boat, trying to push it back up onto the beach. The sand had turned to hard, wet mud, and the boat would not move backwards through it. "Push!" cried Huzzy. "Harder! Harder!"

The tide heard her first and it pulled harder and harder each time Huzzy said the word. Now it was six girls against all the power of the great riptide. They could not see each other or the boat or the tide that they and the boat were fighting. Amidst shouts and cries that were carried off by the wind or drowned out by the sound of the rain and waves, the girls used all their might to save their beloved boat. It was no use. Within minutes the wet sand was pulled out from under their feet and the big boat started moving forward.

"Stop the boat!" Huzzy shouted. "We will lose her! Stop it!" She threw her shoulder against the rough bow, but the boat was pushing her into the water first. She turned and faced the tide and held her back against the boat. Still the boat moved forward, and sheets of water covered her already-soaked body.

"Huzzy!" one of the girls cried out to the darkness. "Where are you? Huzzy!" It was Sarah, feeling along the side of the boat and trying to get to the front where she thought she heard Huzzy's voice over the thunderous water. But before Sarah could reach the bow, the boat pulled her with it, and she had to just hold on and be carried forward, screaming in terror at the greatest force she'd ever fought.

"Sarah!" Annie cried. Her hand grabbed her sister's arm, and now they were both moving and screaming against their will. Allison held on to Annie, trying to stop her.

There was no stopping the shifting sands, the tugging of the undertow, and the steady forward pull on the boat. Huzzy was the first to feel the boat hit the water. The heavy pine logs crashed

head-on with a crosscurrent of waves, throwing her
forward into the hands of the tide. Water swirled
all around her and pulled her under before she had
time to fill her lungs with air. Another push from
waves underneath sent Huzzy up and gasping for
breath just in time to be pulled under again. But
no one could see what was happening to her, nor
could she see them.

Sarah, Annie, and Allison were caught in the
same watery prison, and they held onto the side of
the boat, knowing their lives depended on it. Their
limbs hit against the undersea fans of coral, breaking off sharp bits that stabbed their legs and tore
the skin.

Only Libby and Shawn were left on shore, but
their terror was just as great as they heard the
screams of the others somewhere out in the darkness. Shawn knew what she must do. She must find
her way into the stormy sea and swim out to where
the girls must be almost out of strength.

"I'm going in!" Shawn shouted somewhere near
Libby's ear. "I have to help."

"You'll never be able to save the boat in this!"
Libby shouted back through tears as salty as the
sea.

"Not the boat!" Shawn yelled, already running
towards the sound of the waves. "*Them*!" She ran
as hard as she could and dived over the first wall of
waves that punched her in the stomach. With the

breath knocked out of her, she lost her stroke for a second, but found it with the next wave working in her favour. She could hear screams, and her strong swimmer's arms pulled her closer and closer to the sounds. At last she reached the boat, which seemed to be having no trouble floating on top of the waves, even though it bounced up and crashed down again and again on the water's surface.

Shawn was startled to touch flesh. "Sarah?" she called out.

"No, Shawn! It is I, Huzzy!" She spluttered her words through a mouthful of water. "I must find the girls!"

"I'll swim around to the other side!" Shawn shouted. Her throat was starting to feel the strain of all the shouts, but the roar of the wind and waves gave none of them any choice but to yell their words at each other.

"We will both go!" said Huzzy, pulling herself along the boat's side. New screams made both girls work harder to get around to the other side where now they were sure Sarah and Annie were.

"Allison!" Huzzy yelled, swallowing more water. She had reached out an arm and touched a mass of long wet curls. "Is it you?"

"Huzzy! Thank goodness. Oh, Huzzy," Allison cried as she grabbed onto Huzzy's outstretched arm.

"Annie? Sarah?" Shawn shouted.

"Here!" came a tearful shout. "Over here!"

"Huzzy?" Sarah asked the darkness. "Here we are! Can we let go now? Can we let go of the boat?" Her fingers felt frozen in a grip position, but she needed to open her hands. "Can we let go now, Huzzy?" she cried out again.

"Let go, my girls!" Huzzy ordered. "Let her go now! Just hold onto each other, and do not let go of the hand you hold!"

All together the five girls let the boat slip from their bent and water-shrivelled fingers. The sea took it right away before they could change their minds.

"Swim!" Huzzy shouted. "Back to shore! Do not give up. Swim!"

Shawn pulled Annie's hand and together all the girls struggled to push their way through the whirlpools and swells that reared up around them. For once the water worked with them, pushing them back to where they belonged. Still the noise was deafening, but they didn't need to hear any more than Huzzy's command to swim.

Standing at the edge of the water, Libby had tried to see something of the others or the boat. Her eyes stung from the rain, and they played tricks on her as she tried to focus them in the direction of the screams that came ashore. She saw grotesque mouths opening and closing in front of her, but the sounds coming from them proved they were just waves curling and falling before her. At first she didn't believe the shapes of four girls coming towards her from one of the open-mouthed waves. She blinked the water out and looked harder.

"Sarah!" Libby exclaimed as she saw a face right in front of her own.

Sarah's breath came fast as she fell onto her knees at Libby's feet. "Annie?" she said when she realized her hand no longer held Annie's.

"I'm here, Sarah," Annie said, falling down next to Sarah.

Shawn came next, dragging Allison behind her, but in the darkness, surrounded by the ear-piercing sounds of the storm, none of the girls really knew who was hugging whom. They held onto each other as tightly as they had in the water, and felt comforted by the very number of arms that hugged.

It took a minute for anyone to realize that Huzzy was missing. When Shawn discovered the fact, she quickly turned back to the horrid tide that had already taken their boat and called out. "Huzzy! Huzzy!" Shawn cupped her hands around her mouth and screamed frantically. "Huzzy!"

Now all the girls found just enough breath to add their voices to Shawn's. "Huzzy! Huzzy! Huzzy! Huzzy!" Their cries cut through the night and brought back no answer except more waves crashing and swirling.

"Huzzy!" they all tried again.

A boom of thunder and the night's first crack of lightning answered this time. All of the girls looked up at the sky, and in the blaze of the lightning bolt they saw the silhouette of Huzzy standing on top of the rocky wall of the cove, looking out at the boat that was now the current's only captive.

6
Shawn's Secret

Even the brightest sun didn't disturb the six girls who lay sprawled on the beach in an exhausted sleep. Arms and legs were entangled and covered with patches of crusty, dried sand. All of them had clumps of seaweed, salt, and sand matted in their still-wet hair. The place where they lay was the same place the boat had been before the tide stole it from them. It was as if the ocean had taken too big a bite and spat out what it didn't want. It had deposited them on the sand and left them bruised, scratched, scraped, and battered. They were there. The boat was gone.

When Huzzy first opened her eyes she didn't remember right away what had happened or where she was. She could feel the weight of another girl's arm thrown over her own arm, but she didn't immediately recognize that girl as Allison. In the glare of the morning sunlight the girls in the pile all looked alike. She pulled her arm out from under the sandy arm that covered it and felt pins and needles as the blood rushed back into her hand. As the blood came back so did the memory of being tossed wildly out of control by the waves in the dark ocean the night before.

One minute Huzzy had been holding onto Allison. The next thing she knew she'd lost the grip and was being washed out to sea. All hope seemed gone as she felt herself being pulled away from the island. The water came up over her head again and again, leaving her too little time to catch her breath. Just as she was about to go under for what she thought would be the last time, the seemingly bottomless ocean suddenly had a bottom. She'd washed up onto a reef, and even though the coral cut into her feet, she pushed herself along the jagged ocean floor towards the shore. The reef ended at the rocky wall of the cove, and she was able to walk into the wind and climb out of the tide's strong grasp. In the darkness she could not see her bleeding feet, but a sudden flash of lightning lit up the sea and enabled Huzzy to get one final look at the boat as it sailed away without passengers.

The memories were clear now, and a wave of despair washed over Huzzy as she realized the awful truth: She and the girls were stranded again, and the hope they'd had was gone with the boat.

"Huzzy?" A small voice came from the pile.

Huzzy turned her head to see who spoke. "Shawn," she said.

Shawn spoke softly, not wanting to wake the others. "It's gone, isn't it?" she said. "The boat's gone."

"Yes," Huzzy replied solemnly. "It is. The last thing I recall seeing in the storm was our boat far out of reach. I am afraid the sea has taken her from us."

The talking woke Allison, and she groaned as she pulled herself out from under Sarah's leg that was stretched across her legs. "Uh! It's so bright!" said Allison, putting a sandy hand up to shade her eyes. Everything hurt. Her eyes stung, her skin burned, and her head ached. All the battering from the waves and wind had bruised her arms and legs. She looked at the rest of the pile and saw that all the arms and legs were dotted with purple bruises and gashes with bits of coral still in the skin. Only Libby had escaped such injuries. Allison could see the red-haired girl's freckled limbs looking sandy, but free of cuts and bumps.

Sarah's eyes opened next. "Is everyone all right?" she asked right away.

"Everyone is *here*," Huzzy assured her. "We shall have to see how we all are when we have untangled ourselves from this pile." She pulled herself the rest of the way out and slowly stood up. The weight on her feet sent pains through them as the cuts from the reef opened.

Shawn, Sarah, and Allison stood up, too. Sarah reached out a hand to help Huzzy as her feet gave out. When Huzzy explained what she thought had happened to her, Sarah suggested putting her feet back into the water to soak.

"You wouldn't go back into the water, would you, Huzzy?" were Libby's first words as she woke up. She knew that going back into the water couldn't be a good idea.

"Sarah?" came Annie's voice from the last sand-covered girl lying on the wet beach. Slowly she looked around and worked out what was going on. The storm. The boat going out to sea without them. The waves trying to swallow them. Now she remembered it all. "Oh!" she gasped. "We're safe!"

"But the boat is gone," Libby said.

"And everything in it," Allison added.

Huzzy had already realized that. The tools, the sails, the mast, the nautical charts, and the supplies that were most needed for survival were all gone with the boat. Then a new thought struck her. "The matches!"

When she said the word, the others immediately knew what she meant. Without the matches, there would be no more fires. Without fires they could not cook and they could not see at night. "We must go back to the camp and see what the storm has done there," Huzzy said, shifting the weight on her wounded feet.

All the girls moved slowly as they shook out the kinks and knots that made it difficult to straighten their backs and walk upright. They all looked as bad as the trouble they'd been in. Getting over the rocky cove wall was a slow process, but with each others' help they were able to make it to the other side.

"Look at the beach!" Allison gasped. "It's a wreck!" The usual smooth sand had blown into big drifts that were capped with seaweed, beached starfish, sand dollars, and every kind of shell the ocean had to offer. The "wreck" Allison saw was actually a beautiful gathering of all the sea's bounty and gave the girls a fish-eye view of what usually rested on the ocean's floor.

"It's beautiful!" Shawn exclaimed.

"It is," Huzzy agreed. But as she looked at what the storm had delivered, she couldn't help thinking about what it had taken in exchange: the boat. Her eyes looked up to the camp and saw what she was afraid she would see. The storm had torn everything apart, and from where she stood she could just make out the kitchen area caved in.

The girls walked carefully through the drifted sands, watching out for sharp sea urchins' needles and spiny starfish. As they got closer to what had been their camp, Libby cried out, "Oh, no! Everything is ruined!"

It was true. Their sleeping mats were blown away. The palmetto leaf roofs that had protected them from other rains were blown apart and now dangled down in pieces. What had been neatly organized camp areas were now nothing more than piles of leaves, branches, and odds and ends that revealed that people had been there. The clothes they'd decided not to take hung from branches or lay spread out, wet, on the floor of the clearing. It was a disaster area, and as the girls walked through what seemed like a ghost camp, tears finally came.

There were no comforting words from anyone. They held each other in scratched arms and tried to keep out the painful truth, but it was no use. No matter how tightly they held on, the truth kept coming through: All was lost. All was lost.

Shawn couldn't wait any longer. She broke away from the group and hurried up the beach to her shelter. On the way she found a few sketches that the wind had blown and the rains had soaked, but the coloured pencils had not smeared. She picked up the wrinkled papers and kept going, fearing the worst. Her drawings, her paintings, would they all be ruined? She had been prepared to leave them behind, but she wasn't prepared for them all to be destroyed.

Before she got all the way there, Shawn could see that her white tent was no longer hanging from the plum tree branches. She ran the rest of the way and stopped abruptly when she saw the miracle that had happened. Her tent had collapsed under the weight of the rain and wind, but the paintings on the outside were still clear and bright. The sailcloth had resisted the rains, so puddles of water sat on top but had not soaked through. Shawn carefully lifted one end of the tent and peeled it back slowly. The water ran back off the tent into the wet sand around it. Under the protection of the tent, the piles of drawings and paintings Shawn had left sat untouched by the storm. The tent had saved them all from destruction. Tears streamed down Shawn's salt-covered face, leaving dark tracks in the white film on her cheeks. And in the midst of her crying she felt a strange sense of joy. Once again, the island had proved its friendliness to her, she thought. Her paintings and drawings had been spared. But when her eyes fell on the painting of the boat, her joy was diminished. Now the painting was all that was left of the boat, and she knew that would not be enough to save them. The real boat was gone, and with it any hope the girls had for escape.

When she returned to the main campsite, Shawn found the group sitting on the wet sand. Although the sky above was bright blue and clear, the girls seemed to be sitting under a heavy cloud of doom. Allison sat staring hopelessly out to sea. Huzzy held Libby and rocked her to try to silence her sobbing. Sarah was bent over Annie's legs, carefully picking out splinters of coral that splintered again whenever Sarah touched them. In their torn and tattered clothes the girls looked like the castaways they were, and Shawn stopped believing in the friendliness of the island. No friend would have done this to them, and Shawn knew what she had to do. It was time to tell the others her secret. The boat was gone. Hope was gone. But her secret would give them a new hope, and that was exactly what they needed.

Shawn walked over to where Huzzy was sitting, holding Libby. "Huzzy?" she said meekly.

"Yes, Shawn?" Huzzy replied, looking up at the girl. "And have you seen your shelter? Was it very bad?"

"Well, the tent fell down and everything is all blown and wet, but all my drawings and paintings are safe. The tent fell over them and kept the water out."

Huzzy brightened. "That is good news, Shawn. Very good." For a second Huzzy felt normal, but Libby's sobs took the feeling away. Things were not normal, of course. She looked at her girls and did not know when she had ever felt so helpless. In all the days they had been lost, she'd always felt certain they would be found or would find a way to save themselves. But now, even her own hope was gone. She listened for her father's wise voice to help her as it always did, but she heard nothing this time.

"Huzzy?" Shawn said again. "There's something I have to tell you."

Shawn's earnest tone made the other girls look over at her and listen. "Something happened the other day, and I didn't mention it to you or to anyone." She stopped and tears filled her eyes, which surprised Huzzy.

"What is it, Shawn? What has happened?" Huzzy's island accent comforted Shawn and made it easier for her to say what she had to say.

"Huzzy, you know better than anyone that I haven't been unhappy on this island. For me it's been a beautiful adventure, and I never thought of it as permanent, but only as something we should try to gain experience from and learn from. I love the island and the ocean and everything here. My father told me so many times that to make my painting better I had to experience things. That's how I've seen this whole situation right from the start, as an experience that would make my work better."

"Oh, brother," Allison snarled, looking at the mess surrounding them. Nothing looked beautiful to her. And the experience was one she could easily have done without.

"Let her speak, please," Huzzy said. Libby

101

stayed in Huzzy's arms and had stopped crying when Shawn started speaking.

"I never thought about leaving. I mean, I suppose I always felt we would leave *someday*, but I wasn't looking for ways to leave. I love it here." She paused to gather her courage and then continued. "The other night when I was walking by the edge of the water I found something strange."

"What was it?" Annie asked.

"What do you mean, Shawn?" Allison said.

"Fruits," Shawn answered. "But not fruits from the island. I found oranges and lemons and a lime floating in with the tide."

"Where are they?" Sarah asked. "Did you eat them?"

"Without sharing them with anyone?" Annie asked, not understanding the real significance of the discovery.

Shawn swallowed, looked down at her feet, and finally confessed. She especially didn't want to look Huzzy or Annie in the eye as she spoke. "I took them into the groves, back to the sinkhole where Annie got stuck. I threw them in."

There. She'd said it. Now she waited to hear them all blast her with angry words.

Nobody said anything for a minute. Then Libby asked, "But where did they come from? There aren't those kinds of trees on the island, are there, Huzzy?"

"No," Allison answered instead. "There aren't those kinds of trees on the island. And that's exactly why Shawn threw them away." Allison turned an angry flood of words on Shawn. "How could you, Shawn?!" she shouted. "You knew they had to have come from a boat or ship or something passing by. You didn't want us to see the boat because you knew we'd try to signal it! Right? Aren't I right?" Allison had her face right up to Shawn's as she yelled at her. She looked angry enough to punch, but Huzzy pulled her back.

"A ship?" Libby said. "A ship? Passing by here?" She jumped up excitedly. "Really, Shawn? Did you see a ship?"

"No!" Shawn insisted. "No, I didn't see anything. Just the fruits. Really, I would have told you if I'd seen a ship. I *would* have." All the girls were silent as they glared at Shawn, trying to understand what would have made her hide information from them.

"Don't you care about us at all?" Annie asked quietly. She didn't want to believe that Shawn really would be so unfeeling.

"Of course I care about you," Shawn said, tears springing up. "I care about all of you. Why else would I have gone into the water last night? I wouldn't want anyone to get hurt. I don't know what I was thinking when I threw the fruit into the sinkhole. It was the day we were all having fun with the face painting and swimming. I thought at last everyone was getting used to the island and starting to love it the way I did. So, I just thought it was better not to spoil the mood by telling you all about fruits from a ship that probably passed by too far away to do us any good, anyway. You know nothing can come close to this island. The water is too shallow for ships or boats. You *know* that."

The girls had never seen Shawn react so emotionally before. Huzzy stood up and spoke to Shawn. "You were wrong to keep this from us until now," she said seriously. "But I believe you meant no harm. I know you care about all of us. You certainly proved that last night when you came into the water and pulled Sarah, Annie, and Allison out safely."

Shawn's tears kept falling, but through them she apologized. "I'm sorry, Huzzy," she cried. "I'm so sorry, everyone. I know I should never have done that, and I wouldn't ever do anything like that again. You have to believe me."

Huzzy stopped hearing Shawn in the middle of her apology. She was already thinking of something else. The look of defeat was gone from her handsome black face. The look that replaced it was one the girls had seen before, the look of hope. She put a forgiving arm around Shawn's shoulder and said, "I do believe you, Shawn. And I thank you for telling us now. You have chosen a very good time to share this information, and it has given me a new idea."

All the girls looked expectantly at their leader. "What is it, Huzzy?" Sarah asked.

"We can't start again," Allison said quickly. "We can't. It would take forever. We don't have tools any more."

"That's right, Huzzy," Sarah agreed. "We couldn't possibly start again. We don't have the strength to begin again. Well, *I* don't."

"No, my girls," Huzzy said to the raggedy bunch before her. "We will not build another boat to carry us to another island. But if these fruits that Shawn found were indeed from a ship that passed by out in the channel, then I believe we must find a way to get a message out that far at least."

"You don't mean swim, do you?" Libby said, her blue eyes opening wider than usual. The thought of that water terrified her. In the darkness, when the others were somewhere out there in the water, she had stood on the shore waiting for the waves to come for her. First they had taken the boat, then the other girls, and she was sure she would not be spared. But in the morning, when she'd heard the sound of voices, she was surprised to discover that she'd been wrong all along. It was not for her that the tide's tentacles had been reaching. All it really wanted was the boat! But would it spare her a second time? She wasn't sure about that at all.

"No, Libby," Huzzy told her. "We will not swim."

"What *will* we do then?" Annie asked.

"We will find a way to signal the ships that go by," Huzzy explained thoughtfully.

"But, Huzzy," argued Allison, "no one has ever seen our fires. And we've never seen any ships or boats or anything since that plane flew over the first week we were here. How can we get anyone to see us when no one comes into the shallow waters?"

"I have in my mind that we will build a raft," Huzzy said slowly.

"A raft!" Allison cried, shaking her head.

"Nothing so big as the boat. Just something to carry one person through the shallow straight." She looked into the tired faces of her girls who had been through so much. She expected to see faces empty of anything but despair. Instead, Sarah, Annie, Allison, and Shawn seized the hope Huzzy held out to them and looked encouraged.

"A raft for one person will not be too impossible to build. As long as it can hold me up, I will take our message out to sea." Huzzy was deep in her own thoughts.

"Not you, Huzzy," Shawn said definitely. "I'll go. I'm the one who should go. And I'm the strongest swimmer. I *want* to go."

"And how do we know you'll really deliver the message and not just dump it?" Allison said nastily.

Shawn looked into Allison's green eyes and said, "You'll just have to trust me, that's all."

"How do we begin?" Annie asked, turning the subject back over to Huzzy.

"At the end," her father would have answered if he'd been there, thought Huzzy. "First you must work out what it is you wish to achieve at the end of your task. Then begin with that goal in mind," he would have said.

"We will begin by working out what kind of signal we are able to send. Then the raft we build will have to carry it for us." Huzzy held her chin up high and added one more thing. "Together we shall find a way. And I think we are all together in this, yes?"

"Yes," said Shawn, reaching a hand out to Huzzy.

"Yes," said Annie and Sarah together, adding their hands to Huzzy's and Shawn's.

"Yes," Libby said, putting a willing hand out to the others.

Only Allison hesitated, but as she looked around at the storm-torn mess that had been their camp, she realized she had no choice. "Yes," she finally said.

7
Empty Spaces

The damage done by the storm was worse than anyone realized at first. Their camp and shelters were not the only things pulled apart by winds and ruined by rain. Deep in the groves, trees were stripped of their fruits and the jungle floor was covered in a mash of plums and wild cherries. Some trees were uprooted and lay across paths that had been cleared.

The freshwater pool was overflowing and surrounded by thick mud. Floating in the pool were leaves and broken branches. The ground around it was soggy and frightening to the girls who remembered only too well Annie's experience in the sinkhole. No one felt completely safe going near the pool, so dashes for fresh water were made with the same nervousness felt by a runner stealing a base in a ball game. Maybe they'd make it, maybe they wouldn't.

Even the ocean was changed by the storm. The

place the girls called Conch Canyon, where plenty of conch could always be found, was now an empty, shallow pond. The big shellfish had moved to deeper ocean where they found the sandy bottom more trustworthy. Crabs that used to half hide by the water's edge were scared off by the rocks tumbling away with the pull of the strong tide. Fish that dared to swim at the feet of waders had moved out, too.

The girls were more changed than anything else on the island. Their bodies showed the sorry evidence of the battle with the storm. If some miracle brought their families to the shore of the island on this day, they would not recognize their girls. Nothing about them looked the same. Very little about them *was* the same. The storm that tore everything else apart, brought the girls closer together than they'd ever been. They clung to each other as they surveyed the ruined shelters and camp, and cried until their eyes were swollen. Everything they had built was blown apart. Nothing was more broken down or beaten than the girls themselves. But it was one thing to know they were all in this mess together. It was quite another thing to find a way out of it.

The idea of building a raft was one none of them could face yet. Only Huzzy realized the importance of beginning as soon as possible. Before they had sunk too deeply into the idea of giving up,

Huzzy wanted to get her girls working again to save themselves. Her father's voice was always there lifting her up and reminding her that giving up was not something a Smyth *ever* did. Huzzy took the lead in clearing away the fallen trees, branches, and leaves that covered the camp. When she pushed aside a branch and uncovered part of a shelf that had held dishes from the *Sea Breeze*, Sarah looked up and gasped.

"It's all broken!" Sarah said, pushing a clump of hair out of her scratched face. Through the web of blonde tangles she could see the piles of pieces of dishes that had fallen to the palm mat floor under the shelf.

Huzzy sighed a deep sigh as she saw that not only were the dishes broken, but so was the fireplace area Sarah had made, the table, and all the storage areas. "I think we were much better off being in the water during the storm than being here where the trees fell."

"Great choice," Allison said. "To be crushed under a tree or ripped apart by coral reefs." A shiver went through her as she realized how lucky they all were to have come out of the storm alive. The cuts and bruises and splinters seemed a small price to pay, considering the destruction of their camp site.

Sarah didn't want to think about what might have happened. Her way of keeping unwanted thoughts out of her mind was to fill her head with easier thoughts. Cooking always comforted her, but the kitchen was in no shape for any kind of cooking. "Well," she said, "I think the only thing to do here is try to find whatever isn't broken and see if I can work out how to get organized again."

Now Annie and Libby stood up and looked around to see what they might do to help. Sarah straightened her bent posture and tried to get back into her mothering role. "You girls could help by gathering up any nuts and plums that weren't ruined. We'll need to eat."

The two younger girls ignored their cuts and aches and did as Sarah asked. They collected the few plums that had escaped unharmed and picked up all the almonds that had been safe in their shells. When Annie reached under a branch for a cluster of nuts, her hand touched smooth plastic. She pulled out a tightly covered container that had the Windswept Sailing Cruises logo on it and gave a squeal of delight. "Matches!" Annie exclaimed, holding up the container for all to see. "I found matches!"

"The kitchen matches," Sarah said. "I kept those so we could have a fire in the morning before leaving. There aren't many in there, though. Most of what we had went on the boat."

Huzzy looked over at Annie's find and smiled. "Annie, this is a wonderful discovery. In the midst of this terrible mess you have found some good."

"Well, at least we'll be able to have hot food," Sarah said right away.

"If the fish come back," Shawn added, thinking of the empty conch bed and the hiding places deserted by the crabs.

"They will come back," Huzzy assured her. "Storms come and go, but the fish stay. It is only the poor things washed up on the beach that have no chance to choose."

"Can we put some of them back?" Libby asked. "The starfish could go back, couldn't they?"

Huzzy looked out at the beach that looked like the ocean's battlefield and wondered how much of the beached sea life had survived. "I suppose they must feel as lost as we do," she sighed.

That was all Libby and the others had to hear. All at once they turned towards the beach and ran. Libby started to cry out, "Save the fish! Save the fish!" and the others followed her with the same call.

The girls, who could not yet face saving themselves, attacked the task of saving what they could save, the hundreds of sea urchins, molluscs, starfish, and sand dollars. "Save the fish! Save the fish! Save the fish!" The chant became almost tribal as the girls got into a rhythm that went with a dance of bending over, picking up a shell, and leaping towards the water to return the victim to its rightful place.

"Save the fish! Save the fish! Save the fish!" chanted Shawn as she gathered three big starfish and ran with them to the water's edge.

"Save the fish!" Annie and Libby called out together as they came running up next to Shawn with their hands full of sand dollars.

Once the job was begun there was no stopping. Who would be the one to say one fish would not be saved and another would be? The girls were committed to clearing the sand of the survivors and filling up the sea again.

Huzzy did not help save the fish. Instead she worked on her idea for saving the girls. The raft would not be difficult to make. She was sure of that. The storm had taken the boat from them, but it had also brought some trees down for them to use. She made three piles. One was a pile of medium-sized tree trunks that were around the campsite. Another pile was just small sticks and branches to be used for firewood. The third pile was palmetto leaves to be woven into new sleeping mats and a covering for the shelter. When the area had been cleared and the piles made, Huzzy began lining up tree trunks next to each other. She chose trunks that were close in length and diameter, and when ten of them were side by side they looked surprisingly like the picture Huzzy had in her mind of a raft. As she worked and heard the voices of the girls chanting, "Save the fish!" she had a chant of her own going in her head. "Save the girls! Save the girls! Save the girls!"

When the last living thing was carefully put back in the ocean, the rescuers felt satisfied that they had done their best. Just to make sure that nothing had been overlooked, the girls picked through the piles of kelp and seaweed that lay soggy on the sandy drifts. After finding so many things that belonged to the sea, it was a surprise to find something that had belonged to them: a jagged board from the wreck of the *Sea Breeze*. It was not a board that would be the beginning of anything as was the board Huzzy used to begin their boat. Instead, this board was only a reminder of the end of another storm that had taken another boat from them.

Allison angrily picked up the board and hurled it into the ocean. "You might as well keep all of it," she shouted to the water.

"Why did you do *that*?" Annie asked.

"Why not?" Allison answered. "The tide would have taken it sooner or later, anyway."

Libby knew Allison was right. Always the tide was there as a reminder of who was really in charge of the island and everyone on it. The ocean and its currents stood guard on all sides and would not let anyone on or off the island until it was ready. When the girls dragged their tired feet up the beach and back to the camp, Libby told Huzzy about the board.

"And I didn't see any reason to keep it," Allison said. "It wasn't enough to make a new boat with," she said.

"I don't think you needed it, anyway," Shawn said, looking at the rows of tree trunks lined up side by side. "You've already worked it out, haven't you?"

Huzzy looked at her beginnings of a raft. "I believe I have," she said. "The raft will be big enough to hold two people. You and I, Shawn, will carry our message out as far as we can go."

Shawn started to object. She wanted the chance to prove that she really did care about everyone, but Huzzy wouldn't hear of her going alone.

"Just as I needed you out there in the cove's riptide, you will need me out beyond the channel. We will need each other to make sure the messages are placed securely." Huzzy put a hand on Shawn's hand as she spoke.

"How will we leave messages?" Annie wanted to know.

"And who's going to see them, anyway?" Allison said discouragingly.

Huzzy answered seriously. "If our boat made it safely out of the channel without crashing on a reef, it is possible someone will have seen it. Or if it has washed up on the shore of another island where people are living, perhaps those people will wonder where it has come from and who made it. And do you remember that I marked this island on those charts?"

"Oh, yes!" Libby said excitedly. "When you first showed us that this island wasn't on the charts, you drew a picture of it in the spot where it is!"

"And you even wrote 'Chilas Cay' next to it," Annie added.

"Yes, this is true. I did," said Huzzy. "And *if* the boat got out of the channel, and *if* it did not crash, and *if* someone found it and saw the charts, perhaps someone will come looking for the ones who made the boat."

"Us!" Libby said.

"That's a lot of 'ifs'," Allison sighed.

"Yes, but each 'if' is a hope we must hold on to," Huzzy explained, "and the raft must be built straight away in case someone may be looking after seeing our boat. You must try to find that strength and the will to have hope again."

"I have hope," Allison said. "I hope we can eat something now. I'm so hungry."

"Good," said Sarah. "I'll start making something. There isn't much here, but — "

"But you'll invent some new way to make almonds into a whole meal," Allison said without the sting her remarks like that used to have.

"If anyone can do it, *you* can, Sarah," Shawn agreed.

"I think if anyone can do *anything*," Huzzy added, "we *all* can." She was happily amazed that even though the girls were tired, hungry, and worse off than they'd even been before, they were somehow managing to go forward. Sarah would make a meal, the others would make new shelters, and she would start tying the raft logs together with the sisal ropes left from the boat building.

"Huzzy," Annie said again. "How will we leave those messages you're talking about?"

Huzzy hadn't answered her when she'd asked before because even she didn't know the answer. Now, as the question was put to her again, Huzzy had a sudden idea. "I believe I have got it!" she said, her eyes flashing with excitement.

"What is it?" Shawn asked.

"Flags," said Huzzy, sounding very sure of herself. "Sailcloth flags floating on the flotation cushions from the *Sea Breeze*." Suddenly the idea was becoming clear to her even as the words poured from her mouth. "Yes!" she said. "We will make flags like the wind telltales and tie them onto sticks. We must make many of them and carry them out where they will be in the line of boats. Flags can stay out longer than we can."

Over a supper of fruit, fish, and nuts, talk was only of the flags and messages they would put on the flags. Libby suggested simply saying, "Help!"

Annie had the better idea of putting their last

names on a flag and the name of the island on the other side of the flag. But Huzzy had the best idea.

"We shall put the longitude and latitude lines of where I believe we are located, *and* the name of the island, *and* our last names, *and* the word *help*!"

Before messages or flags or the raft could be worked on, the girls had to finally face setting up some kind of sleeping area for the night. The sun was going down slowly, but the events of the day and night before had made all of them ready to sleep early. The fire from supper was used to light one big home fire in front of the area they now all shared. Not even Shawn wanted a separate place. The group spread out palmetto leaves on the ground to make a sleeping area. Their blankets had blown into the groves of trees but had dried out during the day and could be used again. Clothes that had blown into the groves were gathered into one big pile. No one thought of claiming anything as her own. What was left belonged to all of them.

When at last the place was ready and the home fire was burning brightly, the girls lay down like spokes in a wagon wheel, facing each other. This night was so different from the night before. The breeze was soft; the moon was back, a shining sliver of light; and the sky was sprinkled with stars.

Shawn turned so that she was looking straight up

into the never-ending night sky. "It's so amaz-ing," she said. "All that has just happened to us hasn't changed anything really. The stars are the same. The moon is the same. And even the trees don't seem to miss the ones that fell."

The girls stayed silent, thinking about what Shawn had said. Then Libby had a thought: "Do you think the trees really don't miss the ones that are gone? Wouldn't they feel the extra spaces next to them?" She didn't like to think that life just went on so normally when something or someone was suddenly missing.

Huzzy seemed to understand what Libby was thinking. "Trees are not like people, Libby. I am sure the spaces we all left feel very empty to our families."

"Then why aren't they looking for us?" Annie said, saying the thing that no one had wanted to say in all these months. "Why hasn't anyone come for us?" There had been so many times when Annie had wondered about that. At home she had always felt that her perfect sister Sarah was the one her mother and father loved most. But how could they just forget both of them?

"Oh, Annie," said Sarah immediately, "of course they're looking for us. I'm sure a day hasn't gone by without someone, everyone looking for us. They just don't know where to look."

Allison wasn't so sure about that. She'd thought

about how her mother and father must feel to have her gone. At first she only thought of her father being off on business trips all the time, and she thought he wouldn't even have known she was gone for a week or two. And her mother, who was always yelling at her, anyway, what would she really miss other than having someone to yell at? She thought of her mother alone in that big house, really alone now that she was gone and her father was always travelling, and felt a pang of missing her. All those fights they'd had didn't really matter. Allison knew that if she felt that way, her mother must feel that way, too.

Libby had no question in her mind that her aunt Alice would be doing everything she could to find her niece. But, thought Libby, what more could she really do than just hope and know that her Libby was safe somewhere? Libby made a silent promise to herself. She would stay safe so her aunt's hopes were not for nothing.

Shawn had her own thoughts about how her parents would be reacting to their daughter's disappearance. She knew the dark feelings they would have would come out in their paintings. Every feeling felt in the Kallin house was expressed in her father's large canvases and her mother's miniature ones. Just as Shawn had documented every event on the island in her drawings and paintings, so did her parents put their daily lives into theirs. Shawn tried to imagine her father's paintings during these weeks. Dark reds, black, greys, and midnight-blues. And her mother's tiny paintings would perhaps show a ghost of a girl half disappearing in a cloud, with each scene growing fainter and fainter. Her mother would not give up completely as long as there was even a whisper of a chance that the missing girl would come back.

"They'll always be looking for us," Shawn said softly. Then, not wanting her voice to fade like the image of the girl in her mother's painting, Shawn said it louder, more definitely. "They'll always be looking for us."

"Have no doubt about it, my girls," Huzzy said. With the firelight flickering across her smooth face, she looked around at the tired group and assured them again. "They will be looking for us until we are found." She knew that. Her own father would not be sleeping soundly until his Huzzy girl was home. She had no trouble imagining the tears her Mama Selina would cry into her father's strong chest every night. Huzzy knew that during the daytime Mama would try to be strong for Huzzy's little brothers, Juba and Isaac. But at night her mama would cry, and her father would have to be strong for her. Huzzy also knew that he would spend his days out on his boat looking, always looking to see his daughter's proud eyes looking back into his own. "No doubt," Huzzy said again, "they will not stop looking."

"You seem so sure, Huzzy," Sarah said through a yawn, just before her eyes closed for the night.

"You always seem so sure," Libby said, turning on her side and also closing her eyes.

"And you must be sure, too," said Huzzy.

One by one the girls pulled in closer to each other and fell into the sleep that had been expecting them for hours. Huzzy waited, as she always did, for the last eyes to close, and then turned her own eyes to the stars. They twinkled like nightlights from above, casting a glittering reflection over the treetops. Whether it was drops of rain on the leaves left over from the storm or just the silvery undersides of the leaves Huzzy wasn't sure, but it looked as if the trees were being lit up. She thought back to the day when the plane had flown over and missed seeing them. If the trees had looked like this then, no eyes would ever have missed them. A beautiful vision filled Huzzy's head as she settled back on her mat and stared up at the shining treetops. Maybe the night's lights were playing tricks on her eyes, or maybe she was dreaming. All she could see were bright white lights all over the tops of those trees. It was a beautiful sight that stayed with her all night, even long after her eyes were closed.

8
All Alone

Like birds who wake up chirping in unison when daybreak sounds the morning alarm, the girls woke up all talking at once. Except for Annie. Even with the noise of all the other voices chattering around her, she slept.

"Look at her," Allison said, pointing to the sleeping girl. "And she said *I'm* the one who never wakes up!"

"Ssshhh!" Sarah whispered, going over to her sister and leaning over her to get a closer look. "Oh, no!" she suddenly gasped. "I think something's the matter with Annie!"

Huzzy came over immediately and put her hand on Annie's forehead. It was hot as the shell of a turtle sunbathing on a log. Huzzy did not pull her hand away, but instead pressed harder to make sure of what she was feeling. There was no mistake about it. Annie was burning with fever. Even Huzzy's hand, heavy on her head, didn't make

123

Annie move. Her breathing was even, but laboured. The hot breath blowing over her lips dried them so they were white and cracking.

"What is it, Huzzy?" Sarah cried.

Huzzy didn't speak. Quickly she pulled the blanket off Annie and lifted her limp arm to feel a pulse. The thumping inside her wrist was weak. Huzzy bent her head down and put an ear to Annie's chest as a way of double-checking the heartbeat.

All the other girls gathered around Annie and Huzzy, waiting to hear what Huzzy was going to say. They could see, though, that little Annie was very sick. The fever had dried out all of her skin, and she lay still as a stone, making no sound other than the raspy purr of her breathing.

"Get water!" Huzzy ordered. "Someone get water. She is too dehydrated. We must get some liquid into her."

Sarah immediately turned to the kitchen area looking for a cup that wasn't broken, but through her tears she couldn't see a thing. "I can't find a cup!" she sobbed. "I can't even find a cup for water!"

"Here," Allison said, handing Sarah a bowl and taking one herself. "Let's go to the pool and get it. Hurry!" Allison pulled Sarah, forgetting any of the feelings of annoyance she usually had towards her. Together they ran across the path to the freshwater pool and came back with two bowls of cool water.

"Good," said Huzzy, never taking her eyes off Annie.

"Why is she so sick?" Libby asked. "What made her get a fever?"

As she dabbed water on Annie's dry lips, Huzzy shook her head. "I do not know," she said. "But I suppose it is a miracle that this has not happened before." She parted the sick girl's lips, and with her index finger she swabbed water inside Annie's mouth. Then, she tried to cool her body with the water. Starting with Annie's face, Huzzy drizzled water along her arms, stomach, and finally her legs. That's when she saw the cause of the fever.

"Oh, no!" Shawn said when she saw what Huzzy's fingers had found. On Annie's left leg there was a gash with a piece of coral still in it. The infection was obvious and had seemed to spread out from the wound past its original lines.

"Oh, my Anniekins," Sarah cried, leaning over Annie.

"Sarah," Huzzy said, pulling the girl up. "You must boil some water. I will go into the groves to find what the island people call 'fever grass'. If we boil this grass and can get Annie to drink some of it, her fever will break."

"I'll go with you," Shawn said. "I'll help you find it."

"No, Shawn, I need you to do another job. The raft must be finished now, right away. The flags must be made and fixed on the sticks for the cushions to carry. All these things must be done. We have no choice now that Annie is sick. We must try our best to be found."

"She won't die, will she?" Libby said the unsayable aloud.

"Libby!" Sarah shouted.

While the girls talked about what needed to be done, Huzzy examined Annie's wound more closely. The piece of coral causing the infection had to come out. She did as her Mama Selina had done to her brother Juba when he had brushed against coral and come out with sharp bits in his leg. Putting a hand on either side of the wound she pressed down until the piece came out. Next Huzzy bathed it in water and then tore a piece of her already torn shirt and wrapped it around the wound.

Leaving instructions for Sarah to keep giving Annie water, for Libby to start cutting flags from the sailcloth of Shawn's tent, and for Allison and Shawn to begin gathering whatever rope was left from the boat building, Huzzy went into the groves to search for the fever grass. She was only gone for about half an hour before coming back with her hands full of the long blades of grass. These would be boiled into a tea that could save Annie, *if* the girl could be made to drink it.

Sarah already had the water boiling, and the grass was steeped in it until it made a strong-smelling green tea. Huzzy showed Sarah how to dribble the water into Annie's mouth by turning Annie's head to the side. That way she wouldn't choke. Through her tears that came and went, Sarah sat with her sister every minute, talking to her even though Annie didn't seem to hear her. The sight of her sister looking so lifeless made Sarah unable to think of anything else. She would not leave Annie's side and paid no attention to the jobs Huzzy had the others doing. The sounds of a stick hammering against a log and voices talking softly about cutting the flags all became muffled as Sarah sat with Annie.

Huzzy's hand on Sarah's back brought her out of her trancelike state. When Sarah turned to see who wanted her she was completely surprised to see what the others had accomplished. The raft was finished. It was about six feet by five feet with logs tied by long sisal ropes woven in and out between them. Next to the flat raft were five flags raised on sticks sticking into cushions that would float.

"Oh, Huzzy!" Sarah said in a weak voice. "How did you finish so quickly?"

All the girls gathered around, and Libby answered Sarah. "We did it for Annie," she said.

"Thank you," Sarah barely whispered. "Thank you all." She turned back to Annie and dripped more cool water over her forehead. Still, Annie slept, unaware.

"I am going now," Huzzy announced. "I must go before it gets any later."

"But I'm going with you," Shawn reminded their leader.

"No, Shawn. It is better if you stay on the island. I know both the sea and the island very well. But of all my girls, you know the island best. If something should happen to me, I have no doubt you would know how to make the island serve you well. The others need you here with them. And if Annie should wake and find you gone, I think she would feel very worried. We do not want that to happen."

Shawn understood and agreed with Huzzy. It would be foolish for both of them to go, but the idea of Huzzy out there alone frightened them all. What if something *did* happen to Huzzy? What if the raft took her out but didn't bring her back to them?

"Don't go, Huzzy," Libby pleaded.

"You know I must," Huzzy said, holding Libby's chin in her hand and talking right into her eyes. "For Annie. For all of us. I must."

Huzzy packed up food and water to last for three days, a blanket for warmth and shelter from the sun, and the paddle that had been her crutch when her ankle was injured in the first storm. Everyone helped load the cushions and supplies onto the raft so it could all be pushed across the sand and down to the water. Before Huzzy left she told Sarah again what must be done constantly for Annie. "Water. As much water as you can get into her. The fever grass tea as often as she'll take it. Keep her cooled down and wash the wound with salt water twice a day."

Her instructions, which sounded so final, made all of the girls feel a deep sadness. Without Huzzy they never would have survived this long. She was more than just a leader, she was their hope. Each girl took a turn hugging Huzzy and wishing her luck as they said goodbye. As her father had said so many times when he set out to sail the ocean alone, Huzzy now said, "You have my love," and she knew as she pushed off with the paddle that she had their love, too.

Onshore the girls watched and waved, pushing away their tears so they could see the raft and Huzzy. The sun's brightness made it difficult to see her for very long. Before the current swept her gently out of their sight, the girls saw Huzzy centring herself on the raft and rearranging the flag cushions.

The strength of the current worked in Huzzy's favour. It pulled her out, but not with so much force that she couldn't control the raft with the paddle. She used it as a rudder to steer sometimes. Other times she used it as a paddle. She could see the girls longer than they could see her, and it was with a feeling of excitement that she finally took her eyes off the shore and turned them to the vast ocean in front of her.

The horizon wasn't as empty as it looked from the shores of Chilas Cay. What Huzzy could see from the raft that could not be seen from the beach were the tiny islands that were really no more than a few purple points of rock. One of these small interruptions in the ocean's smooth complexion was blanketed by a flock of sea gulls. "Hey, gullies!" Huzzy called out as her raft was carried by. The water around the island was first purple, then bright green, then dark blue showing Huzzy exactly why no ships or boats ever came this way. The depth of the water changed suddenly and only a flat-bottomed boat like her raft could ever hope to glide across safely. The gulls didn't react to Huzzy's call. Out here where no people ever came, the gulls had not learned to fear or be suspicious of a human voice.

"Gully, gully!" Huzzy tried again as she passed by and came to two other small land masses that were completely bare. The course in these waters was definitely full of obstacles. No wonder no one had come looking for them here. In fact, thought

Huzzy, it was a real miracle that the *Sea Breeze* got as far as it did without ramming one of the rocky tops of the underwater mountains.

As she avoided one of the islands by holding the paddle deep down in the water and pushing it away from the raft, the current suddenly changed and she began drifting backwards. "Now there will be some work to this," she said aloud. She paddled as hard as she could so she would move forward. Just when the muscles in her arms started burning from the pressure against them, the current changed again and she could relax a little bit. Waves lapped at the logs, but the flat raft went up and down easily, floating in the rhythm of the rolling water. As a spray of water came up over her bare leg and cooled her instantly, her thoughts turned to Annie back on shore. Another spray of salty water blew over her, sending a chill through her this time. She pulled the blanket around her shoulders and sat like a passenger on a magic carpet. The raft floated on the water, in charge of itself, moving exactly where Huzzy wanted it to go, out to sea.

As many times as she and her father had sailed all around the Abaco Islands, they had never sailed where she was now. None of the small islands looked familiar to her. None of them was on any charts she had ever seen. She knew any rescue missions would have looked at islands that were closer to the course the *Sea Breeze* was to have taken. Even a storm as wild as the one that blew them to Chilas Cay should not have been able to take them through this channel.

She pulled the blanket even tighter around herself because out on the open sea with the sun getting lower in the sky, the air blew chilly. Now Huzzy realized she would not be far enough out to leave the messages until long after dark. To stay on the raft in the darkness would be too risky. If she fell asleep and the current carried her in the wrong direction she could get lost. Instead, Huzzy sighted the next tiny island and steered the raft towards it. It was a rocky bit of land about four times the size of the raft. In front of it Huzzy could see the water's changing colours. The light turquoise showed her she could step off the raft and walk it onto the rocks. No birds nested here. No sprigs of sea grass grew between the rocks worn smooth by waves washing over them again and again. It was bare, but it would do for the night. She pulled the raft up and tied it around one of the rocks so it would not be stolen from her by the night tides.

Water swirled around the island and wind blew straight across it silently because there were no trees to rustle. Huzzy had never heard silence like this before. The darker it became, the more silent it seemed to grow. She looked out towards the island she had left behind and couldn't see any sign of it.

"No wonder no one has found us," she said aloud. 'We truly are lost on that island."

But in all the time on that island, Huzzy had never felt as lost as she felt right now. She missed her girls. She worried about Annie. And she hoped her own courage would hold out as long as she needed it.

As the darkness swirled around her and she huddled under the blanket, she thought of another island, her home island, Green Turtle Cay. She hadn't forgotten what a night such as this was like at home. After a good supper served by her Mama Selina, her father would gather Huzzy, Isaac, and Juba around him and tell them a story that would sometimes be as simple as reminding them that his own father used to gather him and his sisters and brothers around after supper to tell a story. The point was that nothing had changed so much from one generation on the island to the next. Now, thought Huzzy, it will be I who has a story to tell. And then she thought, If I ever get back to my home, that is.

Before closing her eyes, Huzzy looked once more towards Chilas Cay and tried to send a message: "Goodnight, my girls," she whispered into the wind. "Goodnight."

Libby couldn't stop worrying. All day she'd done nothing but carry water from the freshwater pool to Annie's side. As Sarah followed Huzzy's instructions, dribbling water over Annie's burning forehead and drizzling the fever grass tea into her dry mouth, Libby could only picture terrible things. She needed Huzzy's hand lifting up her chin and telling her some wonderful, comforting thing Huzzy's father had always said. She needed Huzzy's lilting voice singing some happy island song to push the bad thoughts away. She needed Huzzy. They all needed Huzzy.

Without Huzzy there acting so hopeful and so sure, the girls felt more lost then they'd ever felt before. Two voices were missing from the usual conversations: Annie's and Huzzy's. And Sarah's voice had grown so weak from crying that she hardly spoke except to ask for more water or tea.

Allison had gone back to doing what she used to do before they had started building the boat. She sat at the water's edge, watching the horizon for any signs of life. The thought of Huzzy out there somewhere made her feel frightened, alone, and glad it was Huzzy and not her.

Annie's sickness scared Allison. It was the first time any of them had even got so much as a sniffle. Now Annie looked as if she were never going to open her eyes again. Allison was confused by how she felt. She and Annie had always spent so much time bickering with each other. Like sisters, thought Allison, who'd never had anyone but her mother to fight with. As she watched the water Allison realized something that caught her totally by surprise: She was watching the horizon for Annie's sake this time, instead of for herself!

"She's really gone," Shawn's voice said behind Allison.

"Who?" Allison asked, surprised by Shawn coming up so quietly. "Oh, you mean Huzzy," she said with relief.

"She should have let me go with her," Shawn said.

"How's Annie?" Allison asked.

"Same," said Shawn quietly. "And Sarah's exhausted, but she won't leave her side. I was sitting with her, too, but soon it will be time to light the home fire, and I thought you'd want to do that."

"Oh, yes," Allison said, standing up and noticing the sun changing the sky to evening's colours. "Tonight it's more important than ever. Didn't you think she'd be back, though?"

"No," Shawn said. "On the raft there's no telling how long it could take to get out of the channel. She doesn't have a storm pushing her through it this time."

"Yes, and that's the good news," said Allison. "Huzzy's really amazing, isn't she? I mean, to be out there all by herself on a raft. I hope she's all right and comes back soon."

"She'll be all right. I know it," Shawn said with certainty as the two girls walked back to the camp. "Remember what Huzzy's father always said to her and she said to us."

"What's that?" Allison asked.

"He said, 'It's your ocean, Huzzy girl,' and I think when she's out there on it, that ocean *will* be hers and she'll know it."

Allison looked back down the beach towards the water. "I hope you're right, Shawn," she said as they reached the kitchen area that was usually bustling at this time.

Sarah wasn't cooking, and Libby and Annie weren't busy setting the table for supper. Annie lay still, eyes closed, her forehead glistening with the water Sarah was sprinkling on to cool her. Libby sat on Huzzy's mat, holding the picture of her aunt Alice and rocking slightly as she stared at it.

Shawn remembered that Huzzy was counting on her to take her place while she was gone. She knew she could never take Huzzy's place. No one could. But there was one way she could keep the girls' spirits up until Huzzy returned. Without any explanation of where she was going, Shawn ran up the beach towards the place where her shelter had been before the storm tore it down.

The tent still lay in a fallen heap, covering Shawn's artwork. The pictures were what Shawn had come for. In a hurry she swept up the piles of sketches in her arms and last of all grabbed the largest work of all, the painting of the boat. When she got back to the camp, Allison had already lit the home fire even though the sun wasn't completely gone yet. Sarah, Libby, and Allison all looked up when Shawn returned breathless, but with a strange smile on her face.

"What are you doing?" Libby asked. "Why do you have all your drawings and paintings?"

Shawn was already busy spreading out the papers and leaning them up against the trees, rocks, and piles of clothing around the home fire. In careful order, Shawn laid out the pictures that told the whole story of the lost girls, from the very first day on the *Sea Breeze* as it left the quayside in Fort Lauderdale, Florida. It was the first time most of the girls had seen all of Shawn's work. They knew she always disappeared and got lost in her paints and pencils, but only Annie had ever seen all of Shawn's paintings and sketches.

Sarah looked up from her nursing duties and smiled faintly. "Oh, Shawn," she said, looking around at pictures that included herself as well as little Annie and the others. "You have it all there in your work."

"Yes," said Shawn, sounding just a bit like Huzzy. "It is a good time to look at this, yes? If you look at the pictures I think you will know and feel certain that Huzzy will come back to us safely.

See? Look at this one of Huzzy standing so straight and tall at the bow of the *Sea Breeze*. It *is* her ocean, isn't it?"

Libby stood up and examined the pictures more closely. "Yes!" she bubbled the way she always used to. "And look here at the gullies following us on the boat. Maybe Huzzy has found them and they'll keep her company out there!"

"And here's one of Huzzy opening the conch the first time she showed us how," Allison said. "I thought I would be sick when she said we were actually going to eat that thing, but at least we know Huzzy won't go hungry out there."

In the fading light of evening and then the glowing light of the home fire's flames, the girls studied all the pictures and remembered each and every important event. What was very clear to everyone was the fact that Huzzy had brought them safely through days and weeks and months of all kinds of experiences. Now she was alone, but they all had the feeling that it was they who felt more alone than she did.

Only Annie, who still slept and was unaware of Huzzy's absence, was free from missing her. The rest of the girls huddled close together, pulled their blankets over themselves, and said goodnight. As Huzzy would have if she'd been there, Shawn kept her eyes open until the last girl was asleep. Then she looked out at the moonlit ocean and sent a message to Huzzy: "Goodnight, Huzzy girl," she said. "Goodnight."

9
Signs of Life

"Sarah!" a strange voice cried out in the morning's first light. It was more animal than human.

Sarah was jolted awake by the anguished cry, and she sat up with eyes open, listening to see if a dream had howled out her name. She looked around and saw Libby sitting up and looking around, too.

"Was that you, Sarah?" Libby asked.

"No," came another voice from the semi-darkness. Shawn was up looking over at Annie. "It was Annie. I was already awake and I heard her breathing harder. Then she cried out like that."

Sarah looked at Annie, who now slept soundly. It was hard to believe that it had been she who made that strange sound. Sarah put her hand on Annie's forehead and felt the same dry heat of the day before. Obviously the fever grass tea hadn't worked yet. Sarah broke down. "Oh, Annie," she said softly through her tears, "you have to get better. You *have* to get better." The tears fell softly like new morning dew as she looked down at Annie's small form lying on the mat. She watched her sister for a few minutes, silently, waiting to see if she would call out again. She didn't.

Allison still slept and didn't see what the three girls who were awake saw. The morning was more grey than usual with low clouds hanging over the ocean, giving it a sombre olive-green colour instead of the pretty turquoise of sunnier days. It was one of those days that didn't know yet how it wanted to turn out. The clouds might be blown aside as the morning breezes came along, or they might just hang over, threatening showers later. It was too soon to tell, but it wasn't too soon for the girls to worry about Huzzy somewhere out there under those uncertain skies.

To Libby the clouds seemed like a smothering blanket, and she pictured Huzzy trapped beneath it, fighting to keep it off her face. When she looked up, directly overhead, she saw an airhole in the clouds and bright blue sky on the other side of the cloud cover. "Maybe it's clear out where Huzzy is," she said. "Maybe the day starts sooner out there with no trees blocking out light."

"When Huzzy and I were on the deck of the *Sea Breeze* together and the rest of you were down in the cabins, she told me about all the times she and her father were out on the ocean sailing together. I think she probably woke up to a lot of mornings like this. She won't be frightened by it." Shawn believed what she was telling Libby. Huzzy was at home on the water as she was on land. Shawn only hoped that their leader was *on* the water and not *in* the water. The raft looked sturdy, but if the ocean could swallow the *Sea Breeze* as it had, a raft would seem like nothing more than an appetizer.

"But what if she gets lost?" Libby asked. "What if she can't find her way back to us?"

Allison's voice answered through a yawn and a stretch. "That's why we have the home fire," she said. "Morning," she added as an afterthought.

"Good morning, Allison," Sarah said, her attention distracted from Annie for the moment.

"How's Annie this morning?" Allison asked right away. "Is she any better?"

"Still hot," Sarah answered. "The fever won't go away."

"We have to clean the wound and change the bandage again," Shawn reminded Sarah. "Why don't you boil the water for the fever grass tea, and I'll change the bandage?"

"No!" Sarah said more sharply than she meant to. "No. I have to take care of her. She's *my* sister."

"We all have to take care of her, Sarah," Allison said more softly than she'd ever spoken to any of them. "We're all like sisters now."

It was true. When Allison said it, the others all realized how very true it was. They were all like sisters, and in fact, they had all been through more experiences together than most family members go through in a lifetime.

"Only one of our sisters is gone," Libby reminded them.

"She'll be back, Libby," Allison insisted.

"I keep seeing this terrible picture of Huzzy out there in some terrible kind of trouble," Libby cried.

"I know about the pictures you get in your mind, Libby," Shawn said. "But instead of looking at those pictures, try to see my pictures. In all of them Huzzy is strong and sure of what she's doing. Allison's right. She'll be back."

Libby wanted to believe what Shawn and Allison were saying but she had seen what the ocean's tides could do. "I'm sorry," she said sincerely. "But isn't there some way we can make sure she'll find her way back to us? We need her."

"Of course we need her, Libby," Shawn said firmly. "And she needs us, too."

"Maybe Libby's right," Sarah said, looking at Annie and feeling completely helpless. "Maybe we should go after her."

"No," said Allison. "That would be ridiculous. We can't keep sending one after another. Everyone knows that when you get lost you're supposed to stay in one place. We have to stay right here."

"Well, the home fire won't do any good during the daytime," Libby said. "And what if the reason no one has found us is because this island can't be seen from out there? Maybe it's just too low down or something."

The girls fell silent as they each thought about the situation. Huzzy had gone for help, but maybe Huzzy herself needed help now. And what about Annie? How long could they keep sprinkling water on her hot head while trying to give her drops of a tea that smelled like some strange witch's brew? How long could the fever last? How long could *Annie* last?

As the morning slipped away and Annie's condition didn't change, the watch for Huzzy's return intensified. Allison kept her eyes glued to the spot from which Huzzy had sailed. Libby got up all her courage and climbed to the top of the rocky cove wall to watch for the small raft. Shawn walked down the beach to the place where she'd been chased by the shark and tried to see any sign of a returning raft carrying Huzzy back to them. Nobody saw anything out on the horizon except the usual gulls that flew in and out of the low-hanging clouds.

Sarah continued to do all the things Huzzy told her to. She tried to keep her sister's body cool by soaking a cloth in water and wiping Annie's face with it. As she wiped she noticed Annie's breathing changing. First it was the raspy purring it had been all night. Then it speeded up, and her mouth opened as if to gulp in the air. She tossed and turned on the mat, throwing off the drops of water that trickled down her forehead. Sarah was not sure if dreams or discomfort were making her move. All she knew was that in Annie's eleven, almost twelve years, she'd never been so ill. Her mother and father would know what to do, thought Sarah. But then she realized her mother and father would have taken her to a doctor who would know what to do. Well, the truth was if Annie were at home she never would have been jabbed by coral and there would be no gaping wound sending fever through her thin body. All these months Sarah had been playing mother to all the girls. Now, playing was not enough.

"Oh, Huzzy," said Sarah out loud. "Come back to us." Annie moaned and turned a little. "It's all right, Anniekins," Sarah said, pushing a palm across Annie's damp hair. As she continued to sprinkle cool water on Annie, the sky began a sprinkling of its own. It was raining a cool, soft shower that whispered against the leaves of the trees. Sarah pulled a blanket up over her head and Annie's body. She held out her arms to make a shelter for them both until the rain stopped.

Signs of Life

Libby was the first to come running back to the camp. From her lookout place above the cove she saw the raindrops first starting to fall on the water. Each drop was a reminder to her that Huzzy was out there unprotected in this ocean being splattered by raindrops. She turned and carefully climbed down the rocks and ran across the beach shouting, "Rain! It's raining!"

"Come under, Libby," Sarah said, trying to hold up the blanket higher and wider so they all could fit under it.

Next Allison and Shawn came back to the camp with their faces wet from the light rain. Allison looked up at the sky to see if this was one of those showers that would pass by quickly. But no spots of blue peeped through the thick clouds. "I think it's going to be doing this for a while," said Allison.

"I have to keep Annie covered," Sarah said. Her arms were getting tired from holding up the blanket, and the rain was starting to seep through it, anyway.

"My sailcloth tent will work better," said Shawn. "I'll get it."

"Oh, Shawn," cried Libby peeping out of the blanket. "Your drawings! I'll gather them up while you get the tent."

"Thanks, Libby," Shawn called back. She was already halfway up the beach, running into the rain. At the place that was her shelter area, Shawn stepped over the now out-of-date counting wall, and picked up the white, flowered tent that lay in a messy heap beneath the plum tree. The area that had looked so inviting only a few days ago now looked like a place to run away from. She paused only a moment, letting reality soak in even faster than the rain. Her friendship with this island was over. Too many things had happened that could not be forgiven or forgotten. In her mind she said goodbye to this place and hurried back to where the others waited for her.

"I've got it!" she called out, holding the white tent up over her head.

Allison and Libby quickly began helping Shawn set up the tent, tying it to the overhanging palmetto branches. It was only after it was all set up that they realized the tent was inside out. Sarah looked up from her place where she sat next to Annie and saw the pink and lavender flowers Shawn had painted on the outside of the tent. Now they were like a flowered ceiling overhead.

"Oh, it looks so beautiful!" Sarah gasped. "Come in!"

Before the other girls ducked under the white shelter, Libby handed Sarah the pile of drawings. Shawn carried the boat painting inside and placed it where Annie would be sure to see it when she opened her eyes.

"Perfect," said Sarah, looking at the picture. "Annie will love to see it . . ." Her voice trailed off as she realized that Annie had not opened her eyes for two days.

The girls sat huddled together, looking out of the open side facing the ocean. Raindrops beat out a monotonous rhythm, and there was nothing for them to do but wait. They ate plums that Allison had brought in with her and took turns keeping Annie cool. Sarah poured fever grass tea into her mouth while Shawn held her head up. It seemed that some of it was going down her throat, and Annie stirred a little in Shawn's arms.

The darkness caused by the clouds made it difficult for the girls to know when evening had arrived, but the rain made it impossible to light a fire anyway. What no one wanted to say out loud was that Huzzy had not returned yet. Instead they talked about everything except the two things that frightened them most: Huzzy's trip alone and Annie's terrible sickness.

As Sarah looked out into what must have been evening's dusk, she remembered a time like this before. "It reminds me of being at my family's summer cottage at the lake," she told the others. "We had a dog named Kelly who used to chase raccoons and porcupines in the woods around the cottage. One time there was a rainy day like this, and Kelly disappeared. We knew she had to be out there in the woods somewhere looking for her usual animals to chase, but no matter how many times we called, she didn't come back. The rain came down harder, and it got darker, and she still didn't come."

"What happened?" Libby asked.

"We waited and waited, looking out of the screen door into the rain, just like we're doing here, and finally when it stopped raining, Kelly came out from under the porch. She'd been right there with us all along!"

"Too bad we don't have a porch," Allison said. "Maybe we'd find Huzzy under it when this rain stops."

The girls laughed for the first time in days. Then they turned serious again as Libby said, "I hope she's not lost. I hope she can find us again."

"And I hope she was able to put the message flags out where they'll be seen. If she could get out there far enough I'm sure no one could miss seeing those flags." Sarah sounded so sure that the flags were the answer to their problem.

Suddenly Shawn had an idea. "Sarah!" she said. "You just gave me a great idea, I think!"

"What is it, Shawn?" Sarah asked curiously.

"Message flags that are sure to be seen. That's what we have to do for Huzzy!" Shawn was more excited than they'd ever seen her, and her excitement grew as she explained her plan. "We'll use the cloth from this tent and make as many telltales and flags out of it as we can. Then we'll put them up as high as we can go in the trees. If we can climb high enough and put enough of them up there, Huzzy is sure to be able to find her way back here!"

"That *is* a great idea," Allison agreed. "Flags will show up in daylight," she said. "If it ever comes again."

"It'll come," Sarah said. "It has to come. Tomorrow is sure to be the day when Annie's fever goes away and Huzzy comes back."

They talked more about the flags in the trees and agreed that at the first sign of morning, rain or no rain, the tent would be torn up and turned into flags for Huzzy. But now there was no question that night was all around them. The rain pelted the tent, and its even rhythm played like a lullaby to the girls who were all worn out just from the waiting and worrying and wondering when they would all be together again.

No one knew what time it was when Annie's small voice woke them. The rain had stopped, and the clouds must have cleared because moonlight streamed into the tent, glistening on wet leaves on the way in.

"Sarah?" Annie whispered weakly.

"Annie!" Sarah said, sitting up immediately.

Sarah's louder cry woke the others. "What's going on?" Allison asked.

"Sarah?" Annie said again, a little stronger this time.

"Annie!" Shawn cried.

"Annie!" Libby said, too.

"I'm thirsty," Annie whispered.

A sudden wave of confusion filled the tent as all the girls tried at once to find water in the moonlit tent. "Outside," Shawn said, moving out to get it herself. She came back carrying a bowl full of rainwater and passed it to Sarah who held it to Annie's lips while Allison held Annie's head.

"She's drenched!" Allison said, feeling cold perspiration on her hands.

"The fever broke," Sarah cried. "The fever finally broke! Oh, Annie!"

Annie fell deeper into Allison's arms. She was weak, and even with all the sleep, she felt exhausted. She lay very still and just looked up, trying to recognize where she was and work out why they were all there.

"Sarah?" she said softly. "Is it night-time?"

"I think so," Sarah said. "Or early morning. Do you want something to eat?"

"No, I'm just tired. I just want to go back to sleep. Where am I?" Annie looked around and saw the others. "Why are we all in here together?"

Sarah explained everything to her sister, everything except Huzzy's absence. But of course, even in her tired state, Annie noticed. "Where's Huzzy?"

Shawn took Annie's hand and gave her an answer she hoped was true. "She's gone for help, Annie. She's gone to leave messages so that someone will find us and take us home. I'm sure she'll be back soon."

Annie closed her eyes and breathed the even breathing of a peaceful sleep. The others talked quietly about how wonderful it was to have Annie back. With the fever broken, she was sure to recover quickly. In the morning Sarah would feed her and help her get strong again. "Good night, Anniekins," Sarah whispered to the sleeping girl. She was glad Annie could feel peaceful. When Huzzy came back, Sarah knew they'd all be sleeping a lot better. *If* Huzzy came back.

Morning sunlight replaced the moonlight, waking Annie first this time. She felt weak, but she lay still with her eyes open, looking at the beautiful sight above, Shawn's painted flowers on the inside of the tent. Now Annie remembered everything that had happened before the fever caught her in the middle of the night. The storm had torn everything apart, and Shawn's tent had come down. She must have moved it to the camp where everyone else was, thought Annie. She looked around at the others who were still sleeping and felt good to be surrounded by them in this flowered room.

Then Annie's eyes spotted the painting of the boat. It was propped up so she could see it plainly. At first it gave Annie a strange feeling to see it. It reminded her of the fact that the boat was gone. It also reminded her of the sinkhole accident when she and Shawn went looking for paints. And it finally reminded her of Huzzy who had worked so hard with them to keep their hopes up, so they could survive day after day away from their homes.

The other girls could not hide in sleep any longer. The sun had found all their faces and warmed them awake in the gentlest way. Their first thoughts were for Annie, and everyone was pleased to see her eyes open and a smile on her face. With Annie feeling better, Sarah felt better, too. She helped Shawn peel back the tent and untie it from the tree branches.

Annie was too weak to stand, but when she heard about the plan to make flags she volunteered to help with that. While Sarah made breakfast for everyone, the rest of the girls tore Shawn's tent into triangular pieces that looked like ragged-edged pennants. Annie had the job of tying strings to each flag. As they worked together they thought of Huzzy and couldn't stop looking towards the ocean to see if she was coming yet. By late morning there was still no sign of her, but the flags were finished and ready to be hung up in the trees. This was the part of the job no one felt too sure about, except for Shawn.

"I haven't climbed a tree since I was really little," Allison said. "I'm not even sure I remember how."

"I think I could do it if I weren't so afraid of heights," Libby said.

"We'll all have to help," said Sarah. "We'll have to stand on each other just to get a leg up."

The girls gathered their courage and for Huzzy's sake they overcame any fears they had. They worked out that if they piled the suitcases on top of each other, and then added the coolers, or "chilly bins" as Huzzy called them, they would be up high enough to reach the first branches in the pines.

From where Annie lay, propped up against a pile of faded clothes, she watched as one by one the small grove of pine trees closest to the camp became flagpoles adorned with white flags that stood out clearly against the deep blue sky. The breeze lifted them and made the triangular flags flutter. If Huzzy was out there looking for the island from which she had left, the flags would surely let her know that this island was the one.

For the next several hours the girls posted themselves at their favourite lookout spots. Because she had to stay at the camp, Annie sat up higher and kept her eyes looking straight ahead. Libby climbed to the cove wall and watched in the direction of the current. Allison sat at the water's edge. Sarah and Shawn took turns staying with Annie and standing guard up at Shawn's end of the beach. None of them could believe it when the morning was over and then the afternoon started turning to evening without Huzzy coming back.

Sarah made supper and called them all up to the camp to eat. They were silent as they swallowed the crabmeat and fruits Sarah served. The good news of Annie feeling better became overshadowed by the disappointment over the failure of the signal flags. Huzzy only had food for three days, and that blanket she carried would not have kept the rain off. They didn't want to think the terrible thoughts that crept into their minds. And Libby didn't want to see the tragic picture that filled her head. But the truth was: Huzzy was missing.

Libby started crying, and this time none of the girls tried to hush her. The misery fell on them like a load of wet mud. They felt they were sinking in their own sadness. And the strangest thing about the feeling was that Huzzy would have known what to do or say to bring them out of it. Instead, there was no one who could comfort the sobbing group who clung tightly to each other. It seemed there were not enough tears for all the things they mourned. Losing the *Sea Breeze*, losing the boat, losing the camp and shelters they'd built, and worst of all losses, the loss of Huzzy, who had taught them so much and kept them alive for so long.

The breeze that breathed on them felt foreign. Everything felt unfamiliar to them now. They needed Huzzy to save them. So the five girls cried while the orange ball of a sun took its evening dip into the ocean, and they did not see the silhouette against the sun.

"My girls," the voice of the silhouette said.

"Huzzy!" cried Libby.

Through eyes swollen from crying, all five girls faced into the sun and saw the familiar black figure outlined against the orange. They couldn't see her face because the sunlight blinded them, but the voice was unmistakable. "My girls," she said again. "You have done something wonderful, you know. Your flags were my guide back to you."

They didn't wait to hear more. Even Annie found the strength to stand up and throw her arms around Huzzy. All arms encircled her and so it took a few minutes for them to realize she was looking as torn and tattered as the only piece left from Shawn's tent. The questions flew at her. What happened? Was she all right? Did she leave the flags out there? What did she do in the rain? How did she manage to get back to them?

"Hoh!" Huzzy laughed, feeling happier than anyone that she was back. "It was certainly a trip to tell about for years to come," she said. She told about the first day, which led her to the pile of rocks where she slept. She told about the rain that came in the middle of the night and stayed all day. "But I thought it better to just stay where I was until the rain stopped," she explained. "I turned the raft on its side and leaned it against the rocks so that I had a shelter. The cushions with the flags made good pillows to lean against. I spent a second night out there, and you must know I missed you all so very much." She put her arms out and pulled the girls closer as she continued her story. "The next morning, which was this morning, I looked up and realized that I did not have so very far to go to get the flags out where possibly someone might see, although I am sorry to say I saw no boats and no signs of anyone out there."

"So our flags are floating now?" Libby asked.

"Yes, Libby," Huzzy answered. "I did what I went there to do. And then it was time to come back, but the tide had pulled me around so that I lost my sense of direction. I looked for the rocky little island where I had slept but could not find it. All that was left for me to do was to hope that the ocean would be kind to me. I paddled with the current and moved swiftly in a direction of which I was uncertain. My arms ached, but I felt that I would either reach you or perhaps some other island. My food was gone and as you can see from my clothes, the trip was hard on them. At times the sun burned so hot I thought I would catch fire. I thought of Annie and her fever and knew I had to find my way back here. I felt sure the fever grass tea would break the fever, but if it did not, I thought you might need me."

"*Might!*" Allison said. "Now that's an understatement. We *all* need you, Huzzy."

Huzzy smiled at Allison as she remembered back to the first day of the cruise when Allison refused Huzzy's hand to help her into the boat. "Yes, Allison," she said, "we all need each other. And I needed you to help me find my way. From out on the ocean it is very difficult to see this tiny island. From the distance all that appears on the horizon are the treetops, which actually look more like a mound covered with sea grass. But when I saw the flags I knew there were no island trees that looked like that on their own. Even though my arms were against it, I paddled as hard as I could and the tide did the rest."

Everything that only moments ago had seemed so terrible, so hopeless, so sad, was now changed. So much had been lost, but all six girls knew very well how much had also been found. There was never a happier night on Chilas Cay. The home fire blazed brightly as they celebrated the fact that being lost together was very different from being lost alone. Together they would survive another day. And then another. Of that they were sure.

The moon was even brighter than the fire. It threw a spotlight's beam across the ocean, which looked almost too calm on a night of such excitement and celebration. Huzzy sang one of her happiest island songs as they all danced around the fire. As she repeated the verse, she grabbed Shawn's hand and all the girls made a train that wove in and out of the palm trees and finally headed towards the moonlit water. They danced wildly like some happy tribe celebrating a successful hunt. It had been a successful hunt for the girls. They'd watched and watched for Huzzy, and finally she had returned. They followed her willingly down to the water's edge where Allison had spent so many hours sitting with her eyes on the horizon. The dance continued through the shallow shoreline, and they splashed water as happily as babies in a bath. The song grew louder as each girl added her voice to Huzzy's. Nothing could stop the train from moving on. Nothing could still the voices or the feet of the lost group who had on this day really found each other. They wanted the feeling never to end.

Suddenly Huzzy stopped. The happy expression on her face changed to one of complete disbelief.

The others stopped, too, running into each

others' backs as the halt was so sudden. "What is it, Huzzy?" Sarah said, still laughing.

"What?" they all wanted to know, but Huzzy stood with her mouth open and her eyes turned to the sea where the moon's light was not playing any tricks on her.

"A boat!" Libby said breathlessly, not able to believe her own eyes.

Allison shouted as loud as she could, "Help! We're here! Help!"

Now all the voices shouted out at the boat-shaped thing silhouetted against the moonlight. "Here! We're here!" they all cried, grabbing onto each other, jumping up and down uncontrollably, laughing, crying, and shouting again and again, "We're here! We're here! You found us! We're here!"

It was further out than it seemed, and it moved slowly through the shallow waters, but the girls didn't take their eyes off the thing that was coming for them. No voices called back to them, but they were sure their own voices could be heard. Still coming, the boat seemed to be creeping along, but no one on the shore minded. All that mattered was that a boat was coming.

They called out again, "We're here!" Then they listened. At first they heard nothing, but soon they all heard it: a voice.

"Huzzy girl?" said the strong voice of a man.

"Father!" shouted Huzzy. "Father," she said again softly.

As they stood holding onto each other with the fire's light behind them and the moon's light in front of them, Sarah, Annie, Libby, Allison, Shawn, and Huzzy thought the future looked very bright. And they knew, this time they *really* knew, that soon, very soon, they would not be lost girls any more.